# Politicians in Purgatory

**Also by Kirsten E.A. Borg**

*THE PLACE I CALL HOME: What's Wrong
with U.S. and What We <u>Can</u> Do About It*

*BOOKENDS – Alpha & Omega: A Fable for All Seasons*

*RODINA: A Novel of Mother Russia*

*TSAREVNA: The Tsar's Daughter*

# Politicians in Purgatory
## A DocuDrama of the Cold War

**Kirsten E.A. Borg, Ph.D.**

Order this book online at www.trafford.com
or email orders@trafford.com

Most Trafford titles are also available at major online book retailers.

Printed in the United States of America.

ISBN: 978-1-4907-5141-2 (sc)
ISBN: 978-1-4907-5143-6 (hc)
ISBN: 978-1-4907-5142-9 (e)

Library of Congress Control Number: 2014920674

Because of the dynamic nature of the Internet, any web addresses or links contained in
this book may have changed since publication and may no longer be valid. The views
expressed in this work are solely those of the author and do not necessarily reflect the
views of the publisher, and the publisher hereby disclaims any responsibility for them.

Any people depicted in stock imagery provided by Thinkstock are models,
and such images are being used for illustrative purposes only.
Certain stock imagery © Thinkstock.

*Trafford rev. 11/21/2014*

 www.trafford.com

North America & international
toll-free: 1 888 232 4444 (USA & Canada)
fax: 812 355 4082

# CONTENTS

# PREFACE

I intended this book to be a novel. But since the main characters were major world leaders, I could not simply make up what they said and did. So to have them act, react, and interact accurately, I needed to crawl inside their respective heads. This took much research:

- Reading many tall stacks of biographies, autobiographies, memoirs and other thick books about events in which they were involved
- Extensive knowledge of and prolonged visits to the countries they governed
- Understanding of their languages and other cultural artifacts
- How they looked and sounded, their habits and behavior, their goals and motivation, their personality and character

In short, I really got to know these guys. And rather enjoyed 'being' Head-of-State of so many countries. Some more than others.

In a novel, the writer creates the characters. But I discovered my characters as they actually were. The ideas they express are mostly their own, usually in their own idiom. The recorded and discussed events of their lives really happened. What they tried to do, and the consequences of what they actually did, are far enough in the past to be viewed accurately by a responsible historian. Which I am.

Obviously I created the scenario of <u>Politicians in Purgatory</u>. But that's all. I'm not sure exactly what to call this book, but it comes about as close to reality as possible. So if you like to read History, you can believe almost all of what I've written. And find just enough fiction to make it an enjoyable read – even for those who avoid History.

# CHAPTER I

## OPENING STATEMENTS

*The curtain opens on a typical county courtroom. Or so it seems.*

*Enter* Justice *wearing a bright blue robe and diadem rimmed with enlightening rays, carrying an old-fashioned scale and impressive sword. She is tall, neither fat nor thin, neither light nor dark, neither homely nor a beauty. Her dark hair is beginning to grey, and she is definitely a presence.*

Justice: Welcome to Purgatory. I'm Justice, and I run things here. Along with my able team, of course. Of whom more later.

So where's my blindfold? That's a myth. And a very silly one. If anyone has to have her eyes wide open, it's Justice.

And that's why we're here. To find justice for some very powerful people. And – indirectly – for those over whom they had power.

*She places her scale on the end of the Judge's Bench.*

All of the men on trial today were successful politicians. Which means they sometimes had to compromise their principles to get things done. And because they had so much power, they were also vulnerable to hubris. What we are here to determine is where they stand on the scales of justice. Was the greater good served by what they did? Did it outweigh their less-than-honorable compromises? Or did their power corrupt them beyond redemption?

*She rests the large, heavy sword rather casually on her shoulder.*

For some in their line of work, it's easy to decide. For example, there's a special room in Hell, way down on the lowest rung, for Adolf Hitler. Stalin and Mao are a few circles above – but doomed to be roommates for all eternity. The Devil has a good sense of humour, as well as his own brand of justice.

Gandhi, of course, is in Heaven. But he's rooming with Ignatius Loyola, who still has a bit of penance to do. Gandhi is hoping he can hold his own in their perpetual argument long enough to achieve Nirvana.

Most politicans, however, are not so easy to judge. That's why they're here in Purgatory. Our job is to decide whether they go up or down.

*With a powerful swing, she plants the sword in the floor in front of the Bench.*

There's a lot of misunderstanding about how we do things here in Purgatory. We don't punish or torture anybody. We just put people on trial and let them torture themselves. Because one of the rules here is that absolute truth prevails. No one is able to lie. Untruth is simply impossible. So they must not only speak the truth as they know it, but see the truth of their life as it really was. For most politicians, that's more punishment than anyone – even the Devil – could possibly devise.

But before I call them to the witness stand (*looks offstage to waiting defendants*), let me introduce my very able staff.

First, straight from the First Circle of Hell, please welcome the Devil's Advocate!

*(Applause.)*

*Enter* <u>Devil's Advocate</u> *wearing a long flowing red gown with matching cape, and a large red hat featuring two abstract horns. She carries a black pitchfork with diamond-studded tines. On the upper edge of middle age, she is still rather glamorous.*

<u>Devil's Advocate:</u> Greetings from Hell! The Devil sends regards, but is busy making sure that evil people get what they deserve. My job today is to confront the politicians on trial with their worst sins. Most of them are in denial about their mistakes, so it's harder to do than you might think. And it's important to get all this on the record so that – if it comes to that – the Devil can make their punishment suit their crimes. S/He's very dedicated to his/her Vocation, you know. And quite creative. You should see what s/he did to –

<u>Justice:</u> (*interrupting with a collegial grin*) Thank you, Madame D.A., but let's not give away too many of your boss' professional secrets.

<u>Devil's Advocate</u> *returns the smile and, swirling her cape with panache, sits regally in the chair to the left of Justice.*

<u>Justice:</u> And now, just landed from the correctional facility on Cloud #1, please give a round of applause for the Guardian Angel. (*Applause*)

*Enter* <u>Guardian Angel</u>, *wearing a long flowing white gown covered with multi-colored stars, with wings to match. Her halo is huge, tilted stylishly to one side, and she is carrying a small harp. Her hair is white, and she looks like everyone's ideal grandmother.*

<u>Guardian Angel:</u> Greetings from Heaven! God sends regards but is busy helping good people achieve their potential. My job here is to elicit extenuating circumstances surrounding the sins of the politicians on trial. These must be weighed on the scales of Justice, both to determine their fate, and to urge posterity to stop expecting perfection from its leaders. It's important to get all this on the record so that God may send new arrivals to the appropriate rehab center. Contrary to popular belief, people in Heaven don't just sit around doing nothing. Everyone works at becoming who they were meant to be and doing what they should have done.

<u>Justice:</u> Even you?

<u>Guardian Angel:</u> (*sheepishly*) Before I went to Heaven, I was a lawyer.

<u>Devil's Advocate:</u> (*smirking*) We have lots of lawyers in Hell. More, I dare say, than up there.

<u>Guardian Angel:</u> Yes, I'm definitely in the minority. *Flapping her wings a few times, she floats to the chair on the right of Justice and lands gracefully.*

<u>Justice:</u> And finally, from the stacks of the Celestial Library, put your hands together for Clio, the muse of History, who serves as our Recording Angel. (*Applause*)

*Enter* <u>Clio</u> *wearing full Ph.D. academic garb, complete with mortarboard and honorary hood. She carries a huge book containing* a _complete_ record of the _entire_ careers of ALL the politicians on trial. She is ageless and exudes the aroma of an old-fashioned library full of old books.

Recording Angel Clio: Greetings from the Celestial Archives! All of my disciples send regards, but are busy gathering historical truth. As Recording Angel, my job here is to compare the testimony of the defendants with what really happened. This book contains the truth – the whole truth, and nothing but the truth – of their careers. Most of them will be disturbed by what they'll see. It's History as it should be, but never is, on Earth.

_With a sigh, she puts the Book on a large desk in front of the Tribunal, and sits down beside it._

Justice _sits down and bangs her gavel._

The Court is now in session! We now call the following Politicians to answer for what they have done - and left undone. _Bangs her gavel again._

The Court calls Sir Winston Churchill, Prime Minister of England and Advocate of the British Empire.

_Enter_ Churchill _wearing a naval uniform and a huge Admiral's hat. He walks arrogantly to the witness stand, grumbling and growling, and reluctantly sits in the Chair._

Churchill: I protest my presence here, and do not recognize this Court's jurisdiction. You there! (_He imperiously addresses the_ Guardian Angel.) Just ask your Boss. He's an Englishman - he'll understand!

Guardian Angel: (_rolling her eyes and exchanging amused glances with_ Devil's Advocate) Sorry. We've all heard that one before.

<u>Justice:</u> Your petition is denied. But you may now make your opening statement.

<u>Churchill:</u> (*singing to tune of 'Rule Britannia.'*)
    *Chorus:* Rule, Britannia! Britannia, rule the waves!
    The English never, never, never shall be slaves.

    Our Navy circumnavigated the globe
    Upon the British Empire the sun never sets
    Our laws are just, our monarchs constitutional
    We are the greatest, the best race ever bred
    For God is certainly an Englishman
            *Rule, Britannia!*
            *Britannia rules the Waves*

    To all the savage peoples, we did bring
    The blessings of our glorious civilization
    To speak our tongue and wear our clothes and how to pray
    We taught them all this, despite their resistance
    The white man's burden we nobly bore
            *Rule, Britannia!*
            *Britannia rules the Waves*

    When evil Nazis did threaten our shores
    We fought them all and stood alone against the devil's troops
    Through Dunkirk and long nights of blitz we did endure
    We did not falter, we never did give up
    For this was truly England's finest hour
            *Rule, Britannia!*
            *Britannia rules the Waves*

    I led my people to victory
    I often did exhort them with my golden tongue
    Our colonies I did protect with our Navy

I met with Stalin and also FDR
And this was truly Winston's finest hour
 *Rule, Britannia!*
 *Britannia rules the Waves*

When Peace was finally won, I saw a new foe
The Russians took some satellites and seemed to want more
The Iron Curtain I proclaimed and the Cold War
"You must fight them," I told the USA
For God is surely not a Communist
 *Rule, Britannia!*
 *Britannia rules the Waves*

The Colonies were ungrateful, wanted to be free
We were now bankrupt, and our Navy was too small
The Pax Britannica we could not afford
We gave the Empire to the USA
For God can sometimes be American

*Chorus:* Rule, Britannia! Britannia, ruled the waves!
But still the English never shall be slaves.

*Everyone applauds.* <u>Churchill</u> *pulls a cigar out of his pocket, and looks around for someone to light it.*

<u>Devil's Advocate:</u> Purgatory is a smoke-free environment.

<u>Churchill:</u> *(growling)* Go to Hell!

<u>Devil's Advocate:</u> *(smiling wryly)* Good idea. No problem finding a light down there.

<u>Justice:</u> That will do, Sir Winston. You are dismissed for now. *She bangs the gavel.*

*Churchill puts the unlit cigar in the corner of his mouth and belligerently sits in the first seat of the first row of the jury box.*

Justice: The Court now calls Pandit Jawaharlal Nehru, First Prime Minister of India, and Mahatma Gandhi's Chief Lieutenant.

Enter Nehru *wearing a 'Nehru jacket' and a small white 'Gandhi cap'. He mounts the stand with quiet dignity, does a 'namaste' and sits down comfortably in the Chair.*

I'm not sure where I belong, but I will accept the verdict of this court.

*He nods and smiles engagingly at each member of the Court. Obviously charmed, they all smile back.*

Justice: Thank you, Mr. Nehru. You may make your opening statement.

Nehru: (*also singing to 'Rule, Britannia!'*)
    *Chorus:* Rule Britannia! Britannia ruled our land
    And India always always were their slaves

    The English came and took control of our wealth
    They thought because they were white they were superior
    The British Raj was not the Pax Britannica
    We needed freedom to govern our affairs
    For god is surely not an Englishman!

    The British took us into War without our consent
    Liberty and Justice evil Nazis tried to take away.
    'We'll help you fight them only when you've made US free'
    We spent the whole war locked up inside your jails
    Justice is surely not an Englishman!

We practiced Civil Disobedience en masse
We were nonviolent and always turned the other cheek
We went to jail, we hunger-striked for what was right
The British retreated before our moral force
For Gandhi surely was a holy man

And when at last our Independence we won
We also got the awful curse of dread Partition
We were split up into India and Pakistan
So we were stuck with a bloody argument
Is God a Muslim or a Hindu?

When Cold War split the world into hostile camps
I tried to work with both sides to keep my country nonaligned
I mediated many disputes to keep the Peace
I urged the Third World to act as a Third Force
So India could neither be with East or West

My overpopulated country lived in poverty
Science and technology confronted traditional mores
An army to defend from China and Pakistan
To teach people reading in several hundred tongues
To fix all that I'd really have to be God

*Chorus:* Rule, Britannia! Britannia ruled our land!
But India never nevermore is enslaved!

*Everyone applauds except* Churchill, *who glowers at* Nehru, *who tries not quite successfully to benevolently face down his condescension.*

Justice: You are dismissed, Mr. Nehru, for now.

Nehru *smiles unassumingly at the Court, does another 'namaste' and takes the seat in the jury box farthest away from* Churchill.

Justice: The Court now calls General Charles De Gaulle, President of France and Leader of the French Resistance in World War II.

Enter De Gaulle: *Wearing a French Army uniform and kepi on his head, he marches to the stand. Towering over everyone, he sits down with the aura of one who does not doubt his own authority.*

De Gaulle: These proceedings will be more civilized if they are conducted in a proper language. En français, s'il vous plait.

Churchill: *snorts and murmurs loudly.*

Justice: *(banging her gavel)* Order in the Court! Sir Winston, this is NOT the House of Commons!

*(Nods to* De Gaulle*)* Mon General, you may speak in whatever language you choose. It will be instantly translated and understood by everyone else.

De Gaulle: *(saluting)* Merci, Mme de Justice!

Justice: Pas de quoi. *(saluting back)* You may make your opening statement.

De Gaulle: *(singing to tune of 'La Marseillaise')*
    I am the Saviour of my glorious France
    The greatest nation in the world
    We do not need wealth or an empire
    Or a strong force of military might
    Our culture and style makes us great
    We're for peace and moderation
    European confederation
    I said NO to the USA
    When they got bossy and pushed us around

Hooray for Liberté!
Vive l'Egalité!
Marchons
Marchez
All nations to that goal
So Vive la France!

I was a General and I warned of tanks
That Germans used to invade
When my country gave up, I resisted
Stood for France when no one else did
So they asked me to be President
I do not crave power
I really dislike politics
I want no fame nor fortune
I do not even like the French
Too much of Liberty
Leads to Anarchy
I led until
They asked me to quit
But Vive la France!

*Applause from everyone.*

De Gaulle *salutes, marches to the jury box and sits between* Churchill *and* Nehru.

Justice: The Court now calls Comrade Nikita Khrushchev, Premier of the Soviet Union and First Chairman of the Communist Party.

*Enter* Khrushchev: *Wearing a fur hat and loose peasant shirt, he is short and stout. En route to the Stand, he gives each member of the Court a big bear hug and kisses them heartily on both cheeks. Sitting in the Chair, he takes off one shoe and, grinning roguishly, waves it.*

Just in case!

*He smiles and winks.*

Devil's Advocate: *(grinning wickedly)* My Boss would certainly enjoy your company.

Guardian Angel: *(glaring mildly at* Devil's Advocate*)* Are you implying that God has no sense of humour?

Devil's Advocate: *(shrugging)* No – only that the Devil does!

Khrushchev: Since I am an atheist, I believe in neither Devil nor God. But I confess surprise at being in Purgatory.

Justice: Do you dispute its jurisdiction?

Khrushchev: No. I just think it's unnecessary. Any Russian has already lived in Purgatory all his life.

Justice: Hmmm. Well, we will take that into account. You may make your opening statement.

Khrushchev: *(singing mournfully to tune of 'Volga Boatmen's Song'; then exuberantly to a popular Cossack riding song)*
　　　　Famine and Plague
　　　　Stalin and Tsars
　　　　Always Invasion
　　　　Bloody Civil Wars

　　　　Our geography is hard to bear
　　　　Freezing cold and not enough to wear
　　　　Crowded apartments
　　　　Broken tractors
　　　　Peasants who do not know how to read

Gulags and serfs
Vodka and the Bomb
5-year Plans
And Collective farms

Proletariat and Bourgeoisie
Always clashing for Utopia
Communist Party
Leads us to vict'ry
We beat Nazis and we will bury you. *(waves shoe)*

Famine and Plague
Stalin and Tsars
Always Invasion
Bloody Civil Wars

*Sound of galloping hoof-beats, switches to Cossack
riding song*
White nights and dark days
Everyone's a bit bipolar
Tolstoy and Dostoevsky wrote big books
People now can read them just for fun *Yips!*

Singing and dancing
Gymnasts and figure skaters
Athletes winning at Olympic games
Many medals more than U.S. teams *Yips!*

Music and Opera
Shostakovich and Tchaikovsky
Tickets to the Bolshoi could be bought by all
Music schools trained the best for free *Yips!*

We fought the Great War
Sometimes only with our bare hands

Millions of Russians died heroically
But never, never, NEVER again

Sputnik and rockets
Buffer states and great big armies
Nuclear submarines with deadly missiles
Encirclement made us be so prepared

Factories and subways
Built them in a great big hurry
Catching up so people could live better but
There was just too much for us to do.

*Khrushchev reprises the latter verse doing a rather clumsy but surprisingly agile hopak. Everyone but Churchill applauds and whistles and stomps their feet. He bounces enthusiastically to the jury box and sits behind Nehru and De Gaulle.*

*Justice sits down and bangs the gavel reluctantly.*

Thank you, Comrade Khrushchev, for your most entertaining statement.

*Bangs gavel again. The room slowly quiets down.*

Justice: The Court now calls Mr. Lyndon B. Johnson, Senate Majority Leader and President of the United States.

*Enter Lyndon Johnson wearing a very dapper suit, expensive boots, and a huge cowboy hat. He stands very straight, hoping to add a few inches to match De Gaulle's height. Ambling to the stand, he doffs his hat gallantly.*

Howdy y'all. Hope you pretty ladies are doin' just fine.

*He winks flirtatiously at the <u>Devil's Advocate</u>.*

<u>Justice:</u> *(frowning)* Mr. President, I remind you that this is a serious Court dealing with serious matters.

<u>LBJ</u>: Yes, Ma'am, I'm sure it is, but I am an American citizen and am entitled to extradition.

<u>Justice:</u> Here in Purgatory, extradition is irrelevant. From here, you either go up or down.

<u>Devil's Advocate:</u> But we shall certainly keep in mind that you are an <u>American</u> – and all that your country has done. *She winks menacingly at him.*

*LBJ sits down a bit uncertainly in the Chair.*

<u>Justice:</u> You may now make your opening statement.

<u>LBJ</u>: *(Singing to tune of 'Deep in the Heart of Texas')*
    When I was born, the times were tough
    *Clap, clap, clap*
    Deep in the Heart of Texas
    Too many folks had not enough
    *Clap, clap, clap*
    Deep in the Heart of Texas

    And so my vow to right this wrong
    *Clap, clap, clap*
    Deep in the Heart of Lyndon
    Made what I was so very strong
    *Clap, clap, clap*
    Deep in the Heart of Lyndon

For public jobs I soon did run
*Clap, clap, clap*
This was the Plan of Lyndon
And worked long days to get things done
*Clap, clap, clap*
That was the Plan of Lyndon

To get the votes was lots of fun
*Clap, clap, clap*
This was the love of Lyndon
I pressed the flesh till I had won
*Clap, clap, clap*
That was the love of Lyndon

The American Dream for one and all
*Clap, clap, clap*
This was the Hope of Lyndon
Was what I tried to win for all
*Clap, clap, clap*
That was the Hope of Lyndon

I wheeled and dealed to get the power
*Clap, clap, clap*
This was the way of Lyndon
Was in your face and talked for hours
*Clap, clap, clap*
That was the way of Lyndon

The laws I passed for Equality
*Clap, clap, clap*
This was the Dream of Lyndon
Should have made a Great Society
*Clap, clap, clap*
That was the Dream of Lyndon

*Pauses*

To Vietnam we sent some troops
This was the Trap of Lyndon
To save the world from Commie dupes
That was the Trap of Lyndon

But more and more, our soldiers died
This was the End of Lyndon
'Get out of there!' young people cried
That was the End of Lyndon

*Slowly*
A compromise I could not find
This was the Death of Lyndon
My will was gone, so I resigned
That was the Death of Lyndon

*In a minor key*
Mistakes I made, I did not rue
Deep in the Heart of Texas
But what was there for me to do
Deep in the Heart of Texas

*Tepid applause by Court, joined only by Churchill. Somewhat nonplused, LBJ swaggers to the jury box and sits down next to Churchill.*

Justice: Thank you, Gentlemen, for your opening statements. Tomorrow, we shall begin your testimony. Perhaps you are wondering why you are all sitting in the jury box? It's because you will be a jury of peers to each other. But don't bother trying to make deals – that's impossible in Purgatory, too. Just as you must speak the Truth as you know it, you must also decide each other's fate based on the truth as you will see that it really was.

We, of course, will do the sentencing.

The Court is now in recess.

*She bangs the gavel.*

# CHAPTER 2

# GENESIS

Justice: You are all basically here on trial to determine your role in starting or maintaining the Cold War, which was even more devastating than the World Wars which preceded it. Clio, just give us a brief review of some of the havoc it caused.

Recording Angel Clio *turns on the huge screen of her Book of Truth. A large red Nazi flag is being consumed by a raging inferno, to the tune of 'Deutschland über alles' in a minor key. As the swastika goes down in flames, a map of divided Germany emerges. Soviet troops occupy the East, U.S. troops the West. Both sides regard each other uneasily. In the middle of East Germany is Berlin, also divided into East and West. Bullets fly between the American enclave and encircling Russians. Finally a huge wall of ugly concrete is erected surrounding West Berlin. Armed guards glare at each other across the barricades of twisted barbed wire. The Wall becomes a symbol of the Cold War.*

*Next appears the Union Jack, the Tri-color, and all the other national flags of Western Europe. Sousa's 'Stars and Stripes Forever' plays in the background as an American flag flies above, pulling a large pennant labeled NATO. As it expands and settles around the other flags, a Soviet flag appears over the countries of Eastern Europe; its pennant says 'Warsaw Pact'. It, too, descends over the national emblems of its satellites.*

*An iconic mushroom cloud suddenly explodes on the screen. After a long pause, another appears. Then another larger one, followed by an even bigger explosion. The blinding light is surrounded by huge swirling masses of vaporized debris. The lumpy clouds gradually morph into the hydrogen bomb's smooth round ring – like a 'flying saucer' of immense proportions. Guided missiles fly across the scene, some with hammer-and-sickle, others labeled USA. They increase in size and quantity until they fill the entire screen.*

*The screen abruptly divides in half. On one side is a Latin American dictator waving the stars-and-stripes, surrounded by poverty-stricken peasants. On the other side are bearded Cuban revolutionaries chasing plantation owners off their island; in the distance flutters the hammer-and-sickle.*

*On one side of the next scene are U.S. weapons sent to Israel. On the other, Russian arms sent to Egypt. Suddenly, in Africa, a very bloody battle erupts between numerous factions of rebels. Many of them are using weapons labeled USA and USSR, but such is the confusion that who is fighting whom with what is impossible to determine.*

*And then everything becomes China, with Mao's Bomb and cultural warriors pouring off the screen. Mushroom clouds start popping up all over the globe: Great Britain and France, India and Pakistan, Iran and North Korea. And meanwhile, the masses starve, air and water become polluted, glaciers begin to melt.*

*'Stars and Stripes Forever' disintegrates into horrible discord. The piccolo goes ethereal, the brass all play in different keys, the drums*

*lose the beat, the horns lose the afterbeats. Eventually there is only deafening noise that destroys all other sound.*

Justice: Since the havoc started right after World War II, today we need to see what each of you was doing during the Great Wars.

The Court calls General Charles De Gaulle, Leader of the French Resistance.

De Gaulle *snaps to attention, salutes the Court, marches to the Bench, and faces* Justice.

For France World War II was over before it began. Because for us, the Great War was World War I. Most of the fighting then was in France. One can still see remains of the battles – in some places NOTHING will grow – even now. An entire generation of young Frenchmen was wiped out in the horror of the trenches – where the fighting went on and on, and the body counts went up and up. And all for no military gain.

Recording Angel *opens her book to scenes of devastating trench warfare in World War I. In a muddy trench knee-deep in water are exhausted dirty soldiers, all too young and too old to be there. They are ordered 'over the top' and stagger through grotesque wire barricades toward other muddy waterlogged trenches. Equally miserable soldiers return murderous machine gun fire. Some attackers fall dead, others lay wounded on the barbed wire, the rest retreat to their trench.*

*Next day, this scenario repeats, with the two sides reversing roles. Finally deadly poison gas seeps under the barricades into the trenches. The soldiers don hideous gas masks, which transform the weary men into the monsters they have become.*

*Slowly the scene pans out to the huge battlefield. Miles of trenches wind around twisted barricades surrounded by unrecognizable rubble. Thousands of dead warhorses lie rotting. Mud and blood and destruction are as far as the eye can see. Massive cannons exchange devastating salvos which provide grisly counterpoint to the groans of the wounded.*

*Arising from this senseless orgy of death one hears the strains of the Bach B minor Mass.*

> *Kyrie Eleison!*
> *Kyrie Eleison!*
> *Lord, God, have mercy!*

*The choir implores repeatedly, voices wrapping around each other in continuous fugue. The anguished chorus swells until the screen goes blank.*

<u>De Gaulle:</u> When it was finally over, millions of our future leaders lay rotting on the battlefields. Technically we 'won' the first world war, and seized the opportunity to try preventing the Germans from ever invading again. Some of you understand that better than others.

*Looks over at <u>Khrushchev</u>, who nods sadly.*

But the Treaty of Versailles which punished and weakened Germany was not enough. So our exhausted leaders built the supposedly impregnable Maginot Line. And behind it, they hid from reality. Yes, it was an impressive fortification – bunkers and cannon which spanned most of our eastern border. But it stopped at the Ardennes Woods and the Belgian border. And when in 1940, German tanks eventually rolled through those gaps and attacked the Maginot Line from behind, its guns could not be turned around. Those manning them surrendered without firing a shot. And so, the German Panzers rolled on to Paris.

*Recording Angel opens her book. Along the Champs-Élysées, thousands of Parisians are reluctantly lined up to watch Hitler's triumphant entrée through the Arc de Triumph. Their shoulders are slumped, their heads bowed, they are totally dispirited.*

*A German band strikes up a Nazi march, as helmeted troops goose-step down the celebrated Avenue. A wave of disgust passes over the defeated faces of the watching French.*

*A Wagnerian fanfare announces the entrance of the Fuehrer. An open car passes under the Arch; Hitler stands arrogantly in the rear seat, disdain for the cowardly French permeating his entire being. As the triumphant conqueror passes by, there is no cheering. The French try to hide their shame, but many sob silently and make no effort to wipe away their tears.*

*At the end of the Avenue, Hitler faces the Arch built by Napoleon and salutes. 'Siegfried's Horn Call' brazenly proclaims his victory.*

*And then silence. There is no sound of 'La Marseillaise'. Not anywhere.*

De Gaulle: Our leaders, of course, had assumed that future wars would resemble the last one. Only a few of us recognized how the new tanks would soon revolutionize warfare. And when the Germans used the exact strategy I had urged on my own Generals…

*He stops, unable to continue for several long moments. Though his face remains impassive, it is obvious what a struggle it is to retain his military bearing.*

For years, I knocked on everyone's door, trying to convince them of the futility of the Maginot Line. It made me the most unpopular officer in the French Army. No one listened. And I was <u>not</u> promoted.

*He hesitates, tilts his head with understated French irony.*

It didn't take the Nazis long to occupy most of France – and set up a puppet government in what was left. People think that the French Army gave up without a fight. But we are NOT cowards! During the previous Great War we fought heroically. I myself was wounded and captured several times. Always I escaped. *Pauses.* For some reason, I was always caught. Hmmm.

*From the height of his unusually tall body, he scratches his formidable Gallic nose.*

But not all the French wanted to give up, and someone was needed to lead the Resistance. No one with authority wanted the job. It fell on my shoulders by default. Reluctantly I went to England and as the Leader of the Free French, appealed to the citizens of France to resist!

*The stage is suddenly completely dark. One hears the screaming sirens and whistling bombs and blasting demolition of the London Blitz. There is a small and dim spotlight on* <u>De Gaulle</u>. *He is speaking into a BBC microphone. Amidst radio static, his words are heard in France.*

Those who call themselves the French government are negotiating with the enemy for a cease-fire. Is our defeat final? NO! The cause of France is not lost.

*Small sparks of hope flicker in the souls of his people.*

France does not stand alone. For this war is not limited to our unfortunate country. This is a world war, and the world's destiny is at stake.

I, General De Gaulle, call on all French to join me. Whatever happens, the flame of French Resistance <u>must</u> not and <u>shall</u> not die.

*The spotlight disappears. The stage is again totally dark. Off in the distance, one can hear very faint strains of 'La Marseillaise.'*

*Then silence.*

*As the lights come up,* <u>De Gaulle</u> *is again on the stand.*

<u>De Gaulle:</u> To occupied France I sent Agents who organized underground cells to sabotage the German occupation forces. Later, they provided invaluable Intelligence reports to aid the Normandy Invasion by the Allies. Meanwhile, the Vichy Government declared me a traitor and sentenced me to death. There was a price on my head throughout the entire war. But the English Prime Minister did not desert me. He provided safe haven in London, and passage on British ships to far-flung French Colonies. This enabled me to rally them against invasion by the Enemy.

*He nods gratefully at* <u>Churchill</u>.

The American President, however, ignored my existence.

*He glares at* <u>LBJ</u>.

I did not take it personally when FRANCE was snubbed at the Summits deciding the future of Europe. But I did not forget. *He frowns.*

After the Normandy landing, Allied forces slowly reclaimed Occupied France from the Germans. Though the French troops I had organized were a modest part of this effort, we fought harder to free our country. General Eisenhower, therefore, insisted that the French should liberate Paris. Where was I? Marching in front of our troops under the Arc de Triumph and down the Champs-Élysées. There were still German snipers about. And I make a large target. *(A quick Gallic grin and raising of ironic eyebrow.)* Real soldiers of France are not cowards!

*He salutes* Justice *and returns to his seat.*

Justice: The Court calls Sir Winston Churchill, First Lord of the Admiralty, Prime Minister of Great Britain.

Churchill *stands and harrumphs, proceeds to the Bench as though bearing the weight of the entire British Empire, addresses the Court as in the House of Commons. Ignoring* Justice, *he plays to the audience of posterity.*

There would have been no war if people had listened to me. But too many sided with Hitler – or hoped he would invade Russia so the Nazis and Communists would kill each other off. Others just wanted to avoid the bloodshed of the previous war.

*He looks sympathetically at* De Gaulle *in the jury box.*

We, too, lost many of our finest young men on the battlefields of France.

*He looks back at 'audience'.* And so our government gave Hitler what he wanted – over and over. I still remember – with shame – Prime Minister Chamberlain returning from Munich, waving that worthless sheet of paper with Hitler's signature, proclaiming it 'peace for our time.' But the Nazis devoured more and more of

Europe until finally even those desperately supporting this policy of appeasement realized its folly. But by that time Hitler was too strong to stop.

Now, however, people believed me. I was made Prime Minister and belatedly ordered our army to the Continent. But when the French surrendered, English troops were forced to retreat all the way to Dunkirk. And there the bulk of our army was trapped against the sea. But the English people rallied round, and spontaneously sent everything that floated across the Channel to rescue our soldiers.

Recording Angel Clio *shows numerous small craft casting off from docks in the Thames. Panning out one sees an enormous armada of river tugs, fishing vessels, barges, yachts and small pleasure boats. They float downriver into the Sea, crossing the Channel to ports under ceaseless bombardment. From the beaches they ferry marooned soldiers out to the larger naval vessels waiting at anchor. Day and night, back and forth, up and down in choppy waves, the rescuers hoist weary soldiers aboard their small boats and carry them to safety. When, at last, the bridgehead protecting the embarkation collapses, hundreds of thousands of British troops have been saved to fight another day.*

Churchill: And then commenced the Battle of Britain. We braced ourselves to our duty, with only blood, toil, tears and sweat. All alone we fought the Germans. We were ready to fight them on the beaches, fight them in the fields, fight them in the streets, fight them in the hills. We defended our island no matter the cost. And we never gave up.

*On the screen are countless scenes of heroic resistance. Mothers smile and wave, bravely sending their children to the countryside, aristocratic ladies nurse the wounded, Princess Elizabeth drives an ambulance, the RAF flies out against overwhelming odds, air raid wardens marshal orderly citizens to shelters, where they share diminishing rations with a stiff upper lip.*

Churchill: We did not flag or fail, we did not surrender. And truly this was England's finest hour.

*In the jury box, all nod,* Khrushchev *in tears.*

When the will of the English refused to bend to the fury of the Nazi onslaught, Hitler turned his attention to Russia. In violation of the perfidious Nazi-Soviet Non-Aggression Pact, he invaded Russia. They were not ready, and the German Wehrmacht rolled across the Ukraine – almost even to Moscow. The Russians eventually stopped retreating and fought.

Meanwhile we sent convoys of supplies to help them, and I met with Stalin to coordinate strategy. I also met with President Roosevelt to get American ships. When the Americans joined the fighting after Pearl Harbor, I convinced them to focus first on the Atlantic Front. Which also suited Stalin, who wanted a second front to draw off German troops from Russia. Roosevelt promised one in Normandy for 1943 – at the latest. It didn't happen until 1944. Stalin was not pleased.

But we all met in Teheran to start planning how to end the war. And what to do afterward. Later we met at Yalta to close the deal. Stalin & Roosevelt treated me rather shabbily.

*He glares meaningfully at both* Khrushchev *and* LBJ.

As if the British Empire no longer mattered.

*He tries not to see* Nehru's *approving nod.*

Roosevelt thought he could charm Stalin, but 'Uncle Joe' bamboozled him and got a free pass to Poland and Eastern Europe.

Even so, I was grieved at Roosevelt's death. It was not unexpected – at Yalta he was obviously ill. He was a great leader, and a close personal friend. He was sorely missed, especially at the final Summit Conference in Potsdam. The new President tried hard, but he was not up to the job. Truman was a good man, but he was no Roosevelt.

And alas, half way through the meeting, my ungrateful people recalled me. The new Prime Minister was an even worse replacement than Truman. Attlee was a decent man – even though Leader of the Labor Party – but he was no Churchill.

*He snorts, chews on his unlit cigar, haughtily returns to the jury box, and sinks into a sulk.*

Justice: The Court calls Comrade Nikita Sergeevich Khrushchev, Commissar of the Ukraine.

Khrushchev *bounces out of his seat and enthusiastically approaches members of the Court with the intention of again bestowing bear hugs and hearty kisses.* R.A. Clio. *hurriedly opens her Book,* Justice *suddenly hunts for her gavel,* Devil's Advocate *'accidentally' drops her diamond-studded pitchfork,* Guardian Angel *extends her hand to fend off the hug. He grasps it firmly, smiling hugely, then approaches the Bench. It is not his nature to sit still, however, and his speech is frequently punctuated by emphatic gestures.*

All my life, my country has been at war. Our history is, in fact, full of war. Encircled as we are, Russia has been constantly invaded. When we are strong, we enlarge our borders for defense. When we are not, we fight with whatever is at hand.

During World War I, we were sent into battle with no guns. Nothing! Millions of us died at the order of an incompetent Tsar. Finally we gave up and had a Revolution. After a bloody Civil War – and more invasion by foreign capitalist armies – we tried to build a Proletarian Society. With hard labor and enormous sacrifice, we made much progress in catching up with the industrial West. And when Hitler came to power, we knew that we must also rebuild our army. Meanwhile we tried to make alliances with other countries in his path. We approached France – even England – but no one would stand with us. Finally, in a desperate attempt to buy time, we made a Non-Aggression Pact with the Nazis. But even so, we were not ready when Hitler attacked anyway. This time our soldiers had guns, but no bullets.

*He stops in his tracks, and shakes his head sadly. After a long pause, he resumes his perpetual motion.*

But as before, our people fought ferociously. And this time for a cause we believed in – to protect our Nation of Socialist Republics! We heroically transformed our factories into making tanks and artillery, we withstood years of siege, we froze and starved and died. In the tens of millions! This was OUR finest hour!

*He stares at* Churchill, *who harrumphs and looks away.*

And it lasted for YEARS!

Recording Angel *opens her book to scenes of the Russian Front. Across the vast cold expanse of the Russian winter, one sees long trains snaking out to the middle of nowhere, dumping tools and supplies for factories, and old people to build them. The wind screams mercilessly across the steppe. Meanwhile, back in Moscow, thousands of women are digging trenches around the City. In Leningrad, art treasures of the Hermitage are carefully* *and laboriously evacuated beyond the Urals. Hundreds of trucks, dodging bombs, carry insufficient supplies across the Ladoga Ice Road to the besieged city, where starving women pull corpses to cemeteries on children's sleds. On the banks of the Volga is Stalingrad, its ruins the site of fierce and continuous fighting. Russian troops sent into battle are ordered to scavenge ammunition from any of the dead. Despite enormous casualties, the Russian army does <u>not</u> allow the Germans to cross the River. Strains of 'The Internationale' can be heard in between the almost continuous salvos.*

## Arise, O Prisoners of Starvation

<u>LBJ</u> *watches with amazement,* <u>De Gaulle</u> *with sympathy,* <u>Nehru</u> *with admiration.* <u>Churchill</u> *chews his unlit cigar and shifts in his seat.*

<u>Khrushchev:</u> I myself was in the midst of all the worst fighting. At the time, I was Boss of the Ukraine, which is where most of it took place. As Chief Commissar I was on the frontlines as go-between for the Generals there and Headquarters in Moscow. Back then, Soviet Generals were expected to lead at the Front, not behind the lines. I was right there with them at the Battles of Kursk and Kharkov. And finally at Stalingrad, where the tide turned. But it was a long way back to the German border. As they retreated, the Nazis destroyed the factories and dams and railroads we had built during our 5-year-plans. Even worse, they went out of their way to destroy the palaces and treasures of our past. But by the time the Allies landed in Normandy, our armies were already marching on Berlin.

*Outside Leningrad, the enormous palace of Peterhof is being methodically demolished by the retreating German Army. Its elaborate canals and pools are being efficiently filled with the rubble. The huge golden statue of Samson, which dominates the fountains and gardens, is being violently chopped apart and loaded into boxcars headed for Germany. All along their path of retreat, the Germans go out of their way to destroy monuments of Russian culture. The music manuscripts at Tchaikovsky's house are torn apart and defecated upon; Tolstoy's grave is defiled. The factories so laboriously constructed by the 5-Year-Plans are blown apart, the dams and railroads destroyed. Starved and tortured corpses left unburied show ultimate contempt for an entire people regarded by the Nazis as subhuman. Behind the retreating Germans, battle hardened troops fight relentlessly toward Berlin, thirsting for revenge. 'The Internationale' crescendos as they approach Berlin.*

### Arise, O Damned of the Earth

<u>Khrushchev:</u> In my country we don't call it World War II. To this day, it's the Great Patriotic War. Everyone fought. On our land. And lost <u>many</u> loved ones. Afterward citizens – not the government – built war memorials everywhere. And even now they are always surrounded by piles of flowers.

*In the center of a concrete ring is a group sculpture of women mourning dead loved ones cradled in their arms. The aura of tragedy is intense; one can almost feel the blood and tears. Around the pedestal are lovingly laid small bouquets of fresh flowers, many of them left by brides en route from wedding to reception. As the screen pans out and over the Russian terrain, one sees local variations of this scenario in every city, town, and village. None of the statues are of heroic charges; all of them overwhelmingly proclaim that War is truly Hell. A low, mournful woman's voice chants Russian Orthodox funeral liturgy.*

<u>Khrushchev:</u> At least 20 million – maybe even as many as 40 million – of our people died fighting the Nazis. Basically <u>we</u> were the ones who beat Hitler. *He shrugs.* And we, too, resolved

that we would do absolutely anything to prevent this from ever happening to us again.

*He is still, looks intently at* LBJ, *and furrows his brow.*

Why could you not understand something so obvious?

*Bowing his head sadly, he walks slowly and silently back to the jury box.* Nehru *makes room for him in the front row.*

Justice: The Court calls Mr. Lyndon B. Johnson, Majority Leader of the U.S. Senate.

LBJ *immediately starts working the room, vigorously shaking hands and smiling affably. By the time he gets to the Bench, he is on first-name basis with everyone.*

LBJ: My country did not enter the War until everyone else had been fighting for years. Most Americans wanted to stay out of what they considered Europe's problem. I, however, thought we should intervene to stop Hitler. Roosevelt was my mentor, and I followed his lead in getting ships and supplies to England. During the Battle of Britain, I cheered the courage of the English people and urged Congress to help in more concrete ways.

After Pearl Harbor, I led a Congressional fact-finding mission to ascertain the state of the Navy in the Pacific. I sometimes put myself in harm's way and had a few close calls. I was even awarded the Silver Star for my service.

*He pauses, looks slightly embarrassed.* At the time I was pleased to get it, but… I'm not sure I deserved it. Not compared to all that you gentlemen did.

*He looks respectfully at* De Gaulle, Churchill, Khrushchev.

Huhh. That's the first time I've ever admitted that. Quite a strange place you ladies are running here!

*He continues.* Since I had no combat experience, it was decided that I would be more useful in Congress. For the rest of the War, I worked ceaselessly organizing our industries so as to produce enough armaments for all the Allies.

Recording Angel *shows scenes of the U.S. Homefront.*

*U.S. Assembly lines are energetically turning out airplanes and tanks; warships are being launched and sent to England. Most of the workers are women in overalls, their hair wrapped in colorful bandanas.*

> *Don't sit under the apple tree*
> *With anyone else but me*
> *Till I come marching home*

*Amid much excitement, young men volunteer for the armed forces and are sent to boot camp.*

> *He's the Boogie-Woogie Bugle Boy*
> *Of Company B*

*College campuses are devoid of males. American towns seem suddenly populated by young boys – who suddenly become old men. Weddings abound, with the groom in uniform – and no honeymoon.*

> *I'll be seeing you*
> *In all the old familiar places*

*People are exhorted by Mickey Mouse to recycle cans and bottles and newspapers. Gas and nylon stockings and Hershey bars are in short supply and great demand. Hollywood movies show heroic American soldiers fighting valiantly all over the globe. Even Lassie joins the Canine Corps to fight the Nazis.*

> *God bless America*
> *Land that I love*

<u>LBJ</u> *resumes his testimony.* Despite my great respect for President Roosevelt, I had my doubts about his friendship with Stalin. And I still don't trust Communists. But Khruschev's story about all that happened on the Russian Front was really news to me. I had no idea. And to this day, most Americans don't. I wish I had known when I was President... *He looks thoughtful and sighs.*

Roosevelt's death was a great blow to me personally.

*He hesitates, then continues with tears in his eyes.*

He was my hero – and my leader. Our leader...

*A horse-drawn caisson slowly pulls a black draped casket through the broad avenues of Washington DC, followed by a riderless horse with boot turned backward. Color guards of all the armed forces carry flags at half-mast. All march at half-step. The streets are lined with huge crowds of people of all age and race. Women weep openly, waving at the passing coffin with fluttering handkerchiefs. As it is loaded onto a waiting black railway car, one hears the Navy Hymn.*

> *Eternal Father, Strong to Save*
> *Whose arm has bound the restless wave*
> *Who bade the mighty ocean deep*
> *Its own appointed limits keep*

*The train passes slowly through the countryside, lined along the route by throngs of farmers and workers and miners who salute with gratitude. Plainly-dressed people bid good bye to a friend who extended a hand when sorely needed.*

*O hear us when we cry to thee*
*Bless those in peril on the sea*

*And when the crippled body of the President who led a crippled nation through Great Depression and Great War is laid to rest, 'Taps' is sorrowfully sounded. It rises up and echoes across the land.*

<u>LBJ</u> *recovers his composure, and continues.* Harry Truman was a friend. We worked together in Congress. And often shared a drink in Sam Rayburn's office. He was a good, decent man and worked as hard as he could at a job he knew was too big for him. He was no Roosevelt, but he did better than anyone expected.

We Americans were fortunate that none of the fighting was on our home ground. Most of the world was in ruins, but our biggest problem was avoiding a post-war depression. Our Military-Industrial Complex was intact. And we had The Bomb... and had used it.

*On the screen is a blinding fireball which expands into a huge wall of flames. A deafening roar as all in its path is vaporized and obliterated, and then gathered into a whirlwind of debris. It slowly rises and cools into a macabre mushroom cloud, high above the islands of Japan. From this vantage point, one sees how close it is to the eastern coast of Russia. As the cloud invades the atmosphere, its message is unmistakable.*

<u>LBJ:</u> We were unquestionably #1 on all fronts.

*He pauses, and looks thoughtful.*

During the War, the nation pulled together admirably, but in ways that mostly resulted in disruption rather than sacrifice. And because the casualties happened somewhere else faraway, and because we unquestionably WON this War, most of us remember it with almost romantic nostalgia. Just listen to the songs!

> *I'll be looking at the mo-o-o-o-oon*
> *But I'll be seeing you-u-u-u-uu*

In future wars, that's what we expected. And we never understood why it didn't happen that way again.

*With furrowed brow, he returns to his seat, shaking no hands en route.*

Justice: The Court calls Jawaharlal Nehru, Leader of the Independence Movement of India.

Nehru *approaches the Bench with comfortable dignity, wearing his unassuming smile. Everyone – especially the women – are drawn by his effortless charm. He makes a graceful 'Namaste' – and stands on his head. And stays there, straight and steady, his lean body showing no sign of strain.*

*The Court and his peers in the jury box are speechless, trying to decide a proper response.*

Justice *finally breaks the silence.*

A-hem!... Mr. Nehru... The Court is impressed by what great shape you're in... But why are you standing on your head?

Nehru: *(still upside down)* Because that is how my country and I spent the war.

<u>Justice:</u> Ahh, I see. Your point is well taken. Please elaborate. But on your feet.

<u>Nehru</u> *descends and stands.* Unlike the rest of you, I spent the War in jail – a <u>British</u> jail! So did Gandhi and thousands of others. All the best people in India, in fact, were in jail.

<u>LBJ</u> *is puzzled,* <u>De Gaulle</u> *shakes his head,* <u>Khrushchev</u> *is outraged – and shows it.* <u>Churchill</u> *squirms uncomfortably – and bites his unlit cigar in half.*

<u>Nehru:</u> (*not smiling*)
India was dragged into the War by the British. We were not even asked. We would gladly have fought the Nazis. We hated everything they stood for. But how could we fight for freedom when the British would not give us OUR freedom. With even a promise of it after the war, we would have organized all of India into a mighty war effort and fought heroically. But the British refused all our attempts at compromise.

Ever since the first Great War, we had nonviolently protested our subservient status in their Empire. We were NOT the "White Man's Burden." They were OURS – and were bleeding us dry.

*Recording Angel's screen shows one of many nonviolent acts of Civil Disobedience. Led by Gandhi, millions of Indians march to the Sea to make forbidden salt. Indian drums urge them onward, tabla and tanpura beating rhythms that increase in complexity as the size of the crowd grows. Armed with thick wooden batons ringed with iron bands, police line up to stop them.* <u>Nehru</u> *is among the crowd which, unresistingly, walks into the fiercely swinging clubs. Wave after wave are savagely battered and taken to prison. Finally, when the jails are full and the police exhausted, the still surging crowd rushes to the sea, and joyously splashes water onto the sand. As it dries, the salt remaining defies the hated British tax. A jubilant sitar plays a triumphant raga.*

Nehru: We could not stop demanding independence just because of the War. But we did not want to hinder the British war effort. So we decided that individual leaders, one-by-one, would make a token act of noncompliance. In no way would this action interfere with the War. I was one of the first. I made a speech against supporting the British war effort without the promise of Independence. I was immediately arrested, along with thousands of our leaders. We were given long sentences and spent most of the War in British jails.

During previous Independence Campaigns, I had gone to jail several times. So did all the members of my family. But we went gladly – and voluntarily – for a just cause we believed in. Jail is never pleasant, but can bring out one's resourcefulness. Among other things, I wrote books and did yoga. That's how I learned to stand on my head. *He smiles, remembering.*

But Prison during the War served no purpose. It gave Islamic separatists time to recruit advocates for Pakistan. When I think of all the suffering caused by Partition....

*His voice is angry, and only with difficulty does he control his formidable temper.*

For years we were cut off from the outside world, unable to do anything about the injustice the British continued to inflict. The worst was the Bengal Famine...

*There is fire in his eyes, and his voice trembles.* Millions starved to death, despite offers from the Americans to send food. The British Prime Minister declined, claiming that ships could not be spared from the War to transport the food. *He glares at* <u>Churchill</u>.

*The screen moves from village to village in Bengal. Most are deserted, save for piles of bodies – some not quite dead. Jackals and vultures feed on them, leaving hundreds of skulls and skeletons picked clean. The usually inoffensive village dogs have morphed into creatures of nightmare. Wandering in feral packs, they gorge on body parts carried in their bloody jaws.*

*Skeletal figures swarm into Calcutta, falling and dropping on the streets. Stick-like beings huddle in masses. Among the dead are the dying, bent double in agony, stomachs contracted against backbones. Half of the refugees are children, lost when dying mothers in search of food do not return. Abandoned babies litter the streets like stray cats. The steps of orphanages are flooded with foundlings. Little girls are sold to brothels; venereal disease is rampant. On every corner are naked children. Many are picking and eating undigested grain from feces in the gutter.*

*Relief kitchens are inadequate, serving only the same ration given the inmates of Buchenwald. Eventually millions of Bengalis starve to death. Survivors are often too weak to resist the epidemics of cholera and malaria which follow the famine. No one knows exactly how high the body counts are.*

  *Kyrie Eleison*
  *Lord have Mercy*

<u>Nehru</u> *(regaining his composure somewhat):* All of us loved – and revered – Gandhi. But sometimes it was very difficult to follow his teachings. Hardest for me was to 'Hate the Deed, not the Doer.' However, I persevered – and overcame.

*He walks back to jury box, stands before* <u>Churchill</u>, *and extends his hand.*

<u>Churchill</u> *looks at it with disbelief, confused and uncomfortable.*

<u>Nehru</u> *waits.*

*But* <u>Churchill</u> *does not shake his hand.*

# CHAPTER 3

# CHURCHILL (1874 – 1965)

Justice: The Court calls Winston Churchill, Prime Minister of England, to the witness stand.

*Assuming an air of aristocratic disdain,* Churchill *pretends not to hear.*

Justice: Sir Winston!

Churchill: (*in a condescending tone*) Are you addressing me?

Justice: *Slowly stepping down and standing before him, she confronts* Churchill *directly.* It's about time, don't you think?

Churchill: *Unable to resist the force of* Justice, *he reluctantly stands, walks to the witness chair and sits down.*

Justice *returns to the bench and bangs her gavel.* The Court is now in session!

Churchill: For the Record, I shouldn't be here. I am a British Gentleman and can only be tried by a jury of my peers.

*Exclamations of indignation and amusement from the jury box.*

Justice: For the Record, what is a British Gentleman?

Churchill: The epitome of civilized man. Our Empire has brought order, enlightenment, and justice everywhere in its wake.

Justice: Tell us more about this Empire of yours.

Churchill: (*surprised*) You don't already know? Don't you ever talk to God?

Devil's Advocate: The British Empire is not God's area of expertise. My Boss, however, knows quite a bit about it.

Churchill: Harrumph. *He walks over to the* Recording Angel's *screen and takes over.*

It is 1897, the Diamond Jubilee of Queen Victoria's reign. For 60 years, she has been Empress of the largest Empire in the history of the world. It comprises nearly a quarter of the earth.

*One sees the Empire's dominions and colonies scattered all over the globe. Truly, the sun never sets on the British Empire.*

Churchill *continues.* The 19th Century was pre-eminently the British century. We were arbiters of the world's affairs: righting a balance here, dismissing a potentate there, ringing the earth with railways and submarine cables, lending money everywhere, converting pagans, setting up dynasties, winning wars, putting down mutinies, and building bigger and faster battleships.

> *Rule, Britannia!*
> *Britannia rules the waves!*

In Buckingham Palace, Queen Victoria is wearing a dress of embroidered black moiré; ostrich feathers crown her bonnet and she carries a white silk parasol. In the telegraph room, she presses a button which sends her Jubilee message to every corner of her Empire. One sees it flashing through Teheran to India, Hong Kong and Singapore, Australia and New Zealand. Westward it reaches Ottawa, the Cape, colonies of West Africa, strongholds of the Mediterranean, sugar islands of the Caribbean. Everywhere there are statues unveiled and prisoners released, gunboat salutes and garrison inspections, thanksgivings and hallelujahs, grand balls and mammoth feasts.

And into London, amid brass bands and waving flags, pour the gilded emissaries of Empire: princes and sultans, Sikhs and Chinese, Malay ladies and West African policemen – all dressed lavishly and exotically. Joining the parade of beplumed horseguards are battalions from the colonies: gigantic cavalrymen from New South Wales, Hussars from Canada, Carabiniers from Natal, camel troops from Bikaner, head-hunters from North Borneo, Sinhalese and Hausas from the Niger and the Gold Coast.

Amid cheers and patriotic songs and thumping drums, rides the imperial procession: an empress, a crown prince, innumerable princesses, dukes, duchesses, and Indian potentates. The rajahs glitter in diamonds and their ladies are all in gold. The Papal Nuncio shares a carriage with the Representative of the Emperor of China. Guns boom and bells chime, Union Jacks are everywhere – waved by children, draped from windows, flying from towers.

After the Parade, royalty and dignitaries go to Spithead to review the Fleet: 173 ships in lines 7 miles long. Between the huge anchored warships, the visiting grandees sail in an elegant little convoy of inspecting yachts. The Fleet itself is spectacular, painted in a rich black and gold. Rank upon rank, the battleships are lying at anchor.

*Decks are scrubbed, brasswork polished, sailors stand at attention at rail and stern. The scene pans out, multiplying the dazzling sight.*

> *Rule Britannia!*
> *Britannia rules the waves!*

<u>Churchill:</u> It was our right – and duty – to rule the waves and much of the earth. We were <u>called</u> to this noble mission. We spread our principles and liberal traditions so that the future of mankind could be reshaped. Justice was established, miseries relieved, ignorant savages enlightened, all by means of British power and money. And to the peace of the world, we gave the Pax Britannica. Our Navy safeguarded civilization, put out fires on shore, and acted as protector of all merchant ships.

*Nothing on the Seas equals the panache of a British warship. The screen shows one such sailing into a foreign port, all flags flying, Marine Band playing spiritedly on the forecastle, the Captain indescribably grand on his bridge.*

> *Rule Britannia!*
> *Britannia rules the waves!*

*As the glory of the British Navy fades from the Screen,* <u>Churchill</u> *walks proudly back to the witness stand, humming 'Rule, Britannia.'*

*Everyone in the Courtroom is stunned by the magnificent spectacle. Even* <u>Nehru</u> *is speechless.*

<u>Guardian Angel:</u> *(slowly recovering her professional demeanor)* Sir Winston, the grandeur of your Empire is duly noted, as is your dedication to protecting it. We know that World War I dealt all this magnificence a staggering blow. Had World War II not occurred, might Great Britain have recovered its glory?

Churchill: Very likely, yes.

Guardian Angel: It was not part of Hitler's grand design to threaten the British Empire. Rather, you were his role model. He envisioned his own European Empire on land coexisting with yours on sea. Would it not have been in your Empire's best interests to have made a deal with Hitler? A great world war might have been avoided.

Churchill: But at what price?! We were to be the Junior Partner to his dastardly Third Reich! 'Deutschland über alles' was intended to take precedence over 'Rule, Britannia'.

Guardian Angel: But you would still have been powerful – and perhaps retained enough force to keep your colonies.

Churchill: Yes, some of my opponents thought so. I suspect such a deal may have been struck at Munich. But appeasing the likes of Hitler is like feeding a tiger, hoping he will eat you last.

Guardian Angel: But you foiled Hitler's vision of Eastern Europe as his backyard when you declared war over his invasion of Poland. Considering how much trouble Poland has caused throughout European History, why not just let him have it?

Churchill: Because I could not let that ridiculous little lunatic consider himself the equal of the King of England! And besides, it was the right thing to do.

Justice: *turns to jury box.* Gentlemen, what say you?

Khrushchev: Basically it was on the Russian Front that Hitler was defeated. We got some equipment from England and the USA, but most of what we needed we made ourselves. Even though we were already heading to Berlin, we appreciated the

Normandy Invasion. It drew off German troops as did the various campaigns in Italy and the deserts of North Africa. Without all this, it would have taken much more time and many more lives to defeat Hitler. Ultimately I think we would still have destroyed him, but at what cost to Russia? As it was, we were already exhausted. And how would the USA and Great Britain have behaved through all this? Surely it wouldn't have decreased their militant anti-communism. And if they had joined with Hitler to stamp us out? I'm not sure even we Russians could have beaten such a coalition.

*He pauses and grimaces, then adds reluctantly:*

So yes, Sir Winston, the Soviet Union thanks you.

De Gaulle: The French would not have declared War without the British. And while Hitler's main target was Eastern Europe, he could not have allowed the potential threat France posed to his rear flank. All of France would have been shortly occupied, and treated not much better than it actually was during the War. We would have been their colony. They would undoubtedly have seized our fleet in Toulon, and used it to take control of our colonies. Or, since Hitler really didn't want to be an empire of the sea, he might have given it to the English – and given the African territories to Mussolini. In any case, it would have been almost impossible for me to rally French overseas territories without the British Fleet. And for the Resistance, survival would have been very difficult. No, France could not have been France with Hitler as a permanent neighbor. And England could not have stayed England allied to such a monster.

*He salutes* Churchill.

Nehru: If British forces had not been diverted from India, it would have taken us much longer to gain our Independence.

And the Japanese would probably not have been allowed so close to India. Although we cheered them as Asians, we were dismayed by their behavior as conquerors. Might they have coveted the 'Jewel in the Crown' and eventually tried to take it? As badly as the British treated India, I somehow think we would have been worse off with the Japanese. How would they have reacted to non-violent resistance? I think there would have been no place for it in their code of honor. And the British allied with Hitler would have lost their honor and treated us much worse.

But it would have been better if you had let us, too, fight Hitler instead of throwing us in jail. *He frowns. Then shrugs.*

Even so, India is in a better world because you fought the monster instead of becoming his ally.

LBJ: We only joined World War II because the Japanese bombed Pearl Harbor. And also to come to the aid of England. If Great Britain had allied with Hitler, the English Navy would probably not have allowed the Japanese to expand so far into the Pacific. So probably Pearl Harbor could have been negotiated away. No war...but what kind of world would it be? We would have been glad to see the Soviet Commies out of the way, but somehow I don't think we would have cared much for an England that was so chummy with Hitler. And how could we have kept 3 powerful Empires at bay? Seems like eventually we would have gotten into a fight with any of them. *He nods vigorously.*

Hitler was an evil man, and I'm glad we fought him with England rather than against her.

Justice: And Clio, what say you?

Recording Angel Clio: (*shuddering*) There are many possible scenarios. And all of them are terrible. The world would have become an unspeakable horror.

Guardian Angel: Worse than it is now?

R.A.Clio *nods.*

Guardian Angel: So apparently this devastating war you might have avoided was worth it?

Churchill: A War fought by civilized men for a civilized Empire is worth the blood of its noblest citizens.

Devil's Advocate *approaches* Churchill *with relish, ready to make her case.*

For a civilized man, you certainly enjoyed the War.

Churchill: And why not! War is a grand adventure that stirs the blood of heroes. After it was over, I felt very lonely without a War.

Devil's Advocate: I see. *Resting her elbow on the bar of the stand, she leans in.* And why did a 'civilized' British man keep a civilized man of India in jail during most of World War II?

Churchill: (*self-righteously*) Because he and his misguided cohorts were agitating for their selfish goal of independence instead of helping the War Effort. We were protecting India from the horrors and perils of the War, carrying them on the shoulders of our small island. But how could we fight Fascism with traitors nipping at our heels!

Nehru: Objection! Objection!

Justice: The Court recognizes Mr. Nehru.

Nehru: I hated Hitler and everything he stood for. But how could we fight for Freedom in Europe, when India was a victim of oppression? We would have redirected the full force of our Freedom Movement and fought at your side if only you had given us Independence!

Churchill: (*grumbling*) But our backs were against the wall! This was no time to be setting up a new government!

Nehru: But we offered to wait until after the War! A promise of Independence would have been enough!

Churchill: How could we make a promise we couldn't keep!?!

Devil's Advocate: Why not?

Churchill: Because they weren't ready to rule themselves. They needed our help and guidance. Most of them were little more than savages – beastly people with a beastly religion!

Devil's Advocate: (*sarcastically*) So of course it was all right for the 'civilized' British to let millions of these 'savages' starve!?!

Recording Angel *opens her Book of Truth to the Palace of Bengal's British governor in Calcutta. It is appropriately magnificent, built in Greco-Roman style, with white marble busts of Roman emperors adorning its spacious public hall. Surrounded by 20 acres of gardens, it is enclosed by stout walls. Along the entire kilometer-long perimeter are the dead and dying. Every day the governor's troops clear the area, and dispose of the bodies. By the next morning, still more corpses appear.*

*Even so, the social life of the British rich undergoes no change. There is dancing and feasting, luxury and gaiety. There is no rationing. Horse races continue attracting their usual fashionable crowds. Transport is lacking for food, but racehorses come by rail from other parts of the country.*

*Meanwhile, thousands starve in the streets.*
       *Kyrie Eleison*

*The gruesome scene fades.*

Churchill: *(muttering sotto voce)* Lions do not feed rabbits.

Devil's Advocate: There was food available to feed the starving, but you refused to let British ships transport it.

Churchill: Those ships were needed to fight the War!

Nehru: A war that was declared <u>for</u> India – not <u>by</u> India.

Churchill: But the Japanese were threatening to invade India.

Nehru: Then why were Indian troops sent to fight in Iraq, Iran, Egypt, the deserts of Africa – even Greece?

Churchill: Because that's where the British Empire was being attacked.

Nehru: An Empire whose oppression of India made a mockery of its war aims! But even so, we resolved not to impede your war effort.

Churchill: Then why did you and Gandhi threaten to continue Civil Disobedience?

Nehru: This was to be a token act of resistance, limited to a few individuals. We had to somehow affirm our principles. Hypocrisy can never be entirely unopposed. But we clearly communicated this to the British Viceroy.

Devil's Advocate: And how did he react?

Nehru: Thousands of us were immediately rounded up and imprisoned – without having broken any laws. Our entire leadership spent most of the War in jail.

Davil's Advocate: While the leaders of Indian Independence were in jail, what happened to those who favored a separate state of Pakistan?

Nehru: Jinnah and his Moslem League were at liberty to recruit supporters and strengthen their cause. Aided, of course, by the British playing their old game of divide and conquer.

Churchill: Well of course we did! It's standard strategy in defending an Empire. I was not at all enthused by the prospect of a united India – which would then show us the door.

Devil's Advocate: Let's take a closer look at your Empire.

Recording Angel's *screen shows brushfires all over Africa and Asia. Zeroing in, close-ups show British troops with rifles overwhelming natives with spears. Homes are torched and villages leveled. There is much carnage, but few of the casualties are British.*

> *Rule, Britannia!*
> *Britannia rules the waves!*

Churchill: This was necessary for us to pick up the White Man's Burden.

Guardian Angel: Sir Winston, what was the political state of India when the British took over?

Churchill: There were countless constantly feuding princes ruling in luxury over poverty stricken masses.

Guardian Angel: And did you bring order to this political chaos?

Churchill: Indeed, yes! And we introduced them to Parliamentary Democracy. And modern technology. And built railroads all over India.

Devil's Advocate: Sir Winston, as a young army officer you spent several years in India, did you not?

Churchill: Ah yes! And such pleasant memories.

Devil's Advocate: Playing polo and such?

Churchill: Well, yes. But I also did a lot of reading.

Devil's Advocate: Other than your numerous Indian servants, did you interact with the local inhabitants?

Churchill: No, of course not! None of us did! How could so few of us rule so many of them if we treated them as equals? We had to maintain our superiority!

Devil's Advocate: So you invaded India, but made no effort to assimilate?

Churchill: We made an effort not to assimilate!

Nehru: India has been invaded many times over the centuries. But always, there was a fortuitous blending of cultures. Invaders brought us new ideas, they stayed and adopted local customs. This is why India has such a rich and complex history.

Churchill: We brought new ideas, too, and we stayed!

Nehru: Yes, you stayed – but as a conquering race apart!

Guardian Angel: Sir Winston, did all the British live a life of luxury in India?

Churchill: No, I think things were rather difficult for the District Officers alone out in the boondocks. I've heard some of them were quite dedicated to the natives.

Recording Angel Clio *opens book and shows scenes of dauntless District Officers, serving the Raj and its people. They are youngish men in their 20s and 30s, who travel large areas adjudicating disputes and maintaining the power of the Raj. There is much camping out and partaking of village hospitality. None of them know the local language, but their word is law. Most are concerned with bettering the lives of their natives, and build canals and hospitals and such. Though they work long hours, there is time for occasional hunting and pig-sticking. They live in long, rambling bungalows with lots of servants. The sunshine is a welcome relief from the London fog, the oppressive heat is not. Nor are the local diseases against which most have no natural immunity. Corruption is rare, and many a District Officer earns the respect of his villagers. Sometimes he is regarded in benevolent paternal terms. He must, of course, maintain the aloofness necessary for one man to have authority over so many. Marriage is discouraged until retirement, so few have wives. The distance between Districts and peers is long. It is a lonely life.*

Devil's Advocate: While you're at it, Clio, show them Rajpath in New Delhi.

*An aerial view shows the enormous Palace of the Viceroy, a massive square with multiple courtyards, crowned by a huge dome inspired by the Pantheon of Rome, surrounded by extensive grids of gardens, canals, and fountains. The building itself is heavily classical, its massive pillars emphasizing power and imperial authority. Numerous superficial Indian adornments have been reluctantly added. Inside are 340 rooms, the biggest of which is Durbur Hall, where the Viceroy and his Lady hold court. It is directly under the dome; a 2-ton chandelier hangs overhead from a 33-meter height. Near the throne are marble lions spilling water into large alabaster basins. Surrounding the whole 320 acres is an outer wall decorated with elephants.*

## Rule, Britannia

*Outside the front gate, Rajpath is flanked by 2 adjacent blocks of the Secretariat Building, which houses various officials of the Raj. These, too, are large and basically classical, with lots of pillars and domes; several Indian decorations are tacked on. Between these stately structures, Rajpath extends for miles, lined with huge lawns, canals, and rows of trees. At its end, one sees the India Gate, a Napoleonic triumphal arch crowned by a shallow Mughal dome. Off in the distance the Gate appears small, but as one approaches, one feels dwarfed by its magnitude. On Rajpath, British troops parade, reviewing their colors and guarding the other powerful accoutrements of the Raj.*

Devil's Advocate: This was built right before World War I, was it not?

Churchill: True. Impressive, is it not?

Devil's Advocate: And anyone building something like this has no intention of leaving, right?

Churchill: Of course! How could we leave? We had no intention of casting away that most truly bright precious jewel in the Crown of the King, which, more than all our dominions and dependencies, constituted the glory and strength of our Empire. And I did not become the King's First Minister to preside over the liquidation of the British Empire.

Devil's Advocate: But you did.

Churchill: (*sadly*) And that was the end. One by one, our other colonies left us.

Recording Angel *shows maps on which are demarcated numerous colonies in Africa and Asia. One by one, close-ups show ceremonies in which the Union Jack is lowered, replaced by the flag of a newly independent country. The departure of British troops is accompanied by much cheering – but no violence. Panning back out to the map, the colonies of the British Raj disappear.*

Churchill *is close to tears.*

Justice: The Court will recess until after lunch.

Churchill *gratefully leaves the witness stand and exits the stage.*

*Pause*

*The stage darkens long enough for* Churchill *to recover his usual persona.*

*As the set lightens again, after the recess, he is back on the witness stand.*

Devil's Advocate *approaches him with a somewhat sympathetic mien.*

As with so many other empires, World War I literally broke the British. But you hung in there until World War II finished the job.

Churchill *is silent, shifting uncomfortably in his chair.*

Justice: Remember, Sir Winston, that here in Purgatory you must tell the truth.

Churchill: (*growling*) Punishment so soon?

Devil's Advocate: For some, truth is Hell.

Churchill: (*glowering at her*) Yes, we were broke! But the British Mystique allowed us to act as though we weren't. Why else was I allowed to participate at Teheran and Yalta as an equal?

Devil's Advocate: And when Stalin and FDR got too chummy and started ignoring you?

Churchill: I used the time-honored tradition of divide-and-conquer. We British are good at that. *Chuckles.* Besides, I hate those damn Commies! Always did!

Devil's Advocate: And what happened to the Empire?

Churchill: I passed it on to the Americans. They, at least, were kin. And – sort of – spoke our language.

Devil's Advocate: And that is why you built the image of the 'Iron Curtain'?

*The Courtroom morphs into the crowded chapel of a small Midwestern college. On the dais stands* Churchill, *who has just been awarded an honorary degree. After an introduction by President Truman,* <u>Churchill</u> *proffers thanks with his usual eloquence and delights the worshipful audience with his trademark wit.*

Perhaps no one has ever passed so few examinations and received so many degrees.

*Appreciative laughter*

*Then he gets down to business.*

I appreciate the honor of addressing this kindred nation, as well as my own countrymen across the ocean, and perhaps some other countries too. Opportunity is clear and shining for both our countries. To reject it or ignore it will bring upon us all the long reproaches of the aftertime.

We cannot be blind to the fact that the liberties enjoyed by citizens throughout the United States and the British Empire are not valid in a considerable number of countries, some of which are very powerful. The people of any country have the right to choose the form of government under which they dwell. Freedom of speech and thought should reign. Courts of justice should administer laws which have received the broad assent of large majorities or are consecrated by time and custom. So here is the message of the British and American peoples to mankind: Let us preach what we practice – and let us practice what we preach.

*Unable to restrain himself,* <u>Nehru</u> *strides up the chapel aisle protesting.*

Yes, and let us start with India!

<u>Churchill</u> *completely ignores him, as do the assembled representatives of academia. To them, he is invisible.*

*As he disappears,* <u>Churchill</u> *continues.*

A shadow has fallen upon the scenes so lately lighted by the Allied victory. Nobody knows what Soviet Russia intends to do in the immediate future, or what are the limits, if any, to their expansive and proselytizing tendencies. From Stettin in the Baltic to Trieste in the Adriatic, an *iron curtain* has descended across the Continent. Behind that line lie all the capitals of the ancient states of Central and Eastern Europe, subject to Soviet influence. The Communist parties in all these states are seeking to obtain totalitarian control. Police governments are prevailing in nearly every case, and there is no true democracy.

In a great number of other countries far from the Russian frontiers, Communist fifth columns work in obedience to the Communist center and constitute a growing peril to Christian civilization. And from what I have seen of our Russian Allies during the war, I am convinced that there is nothing for which they have less respect than for military weakness.

Now I come to the crux of what I have traveled here to say. Neither the sure prevention of war, nor the continuous rise of just world organization will be gained without a special relationship between the British Commonwealth and the United States of America. Last time, before WWII, I saw it all coming and I cried aloud to the world, but no one would listen. One by one we were all sucked into the awful whirlpool. We must not let it happen again!

<u>Khrushchev</u> *now charges up the aisle, protesting vehemently.*

And we, too, will not let it happen again! We will resist the evil of your Imperialism!

*He, too, is invisible to the rapt audience.*

*He disappears as* <u>Churchill</u> *continues.*

If the English-speaking Commonwealth be added to that of the United States in the air, on the sea, all over the globe, there will be no quivering, precarious balance of power to offer its temptation to ambition or adventure. If we walk forward in sedate and sober strength seeking no one's land or treasure, seeking to lay no arbitrary control; if all British moral and material forces and convictions are joined with your own in fraternal association, the highroads of the future will be clear, not only for our time, but for a century to come.

*There is thunderous applause.*

*But on one end of the back pew* <u>LBJ</u> *sits, scratching his head thoughtfully.*

Hmm, I wonder who's going to pay for all this. The Brits are broke.

*On the other end sits* <u>De Gaulle</u>, *also looking pensive.*

Hmm, what about France?!

*The chapel re-morphs into the Courtroom.*

<u>Devil's Advocate:</u> So you pitted the Americans and Russians against each other. Was that really necessary?

Churchill: The Americans were naïve and thought good relations were possible with Stalin. They didn't understand that such effort was like wooing a crocodile. You don't know whether to tickle it under the chin or beat it over the head. And when it opens its mouth, you can't tell whether it's trying to smile or preparing to eat you up. The Americans needed to be warned.

And besides, how else could the glory of England be preserved.

*In the background, one hears 'God Save the King'.*

Churchill *stands respectfully and resolutely.* There <u>must</u> <u>always</u> be an England.

No matter what!

*The stage darkens.*

# CHAPTER 4

# NEHRU (1889 – 1964)

<u>Justice:</u> The Court calls Jawaharlal Nehru, Prime Minister of India, to the Witness Stand.

<u>Nehru:</u> *Completely at ease, he sits in the Chair beside* <u>Justice</u> *and leans slightly forward with relaxed attention.*

May I say how much I appreciate the personnel of Purgatory? *He smiles.* I have always enjoyed the company of beautiful women who are intelligent.

<u>Justice:</u> *(surprised but not displeased)*
Well – uh – thank you. But flattery is not the norm here.

<u>Nehru:</u> But here, one must always tell the truth – which is never flattery.

*He smiles again. They all take it down a notch.*

<u>Guardian Angel</u> *approaches, returning his smile.*

Mr. Nehru, this wasn't always your customary mode of dress.

*She indicates the 'Nehru jacket' and the white 'Gandhi cap'.*

Nehru: (*in impeccable English*)
Yes, I used to be an Anglophile. In some ways I still am. Why else would I have insisted on a Parliamentary Democracy for India? After Independence, it would have been much easier to simply move into the Viceroy's Palace and tell everyone what to do.
*He laughs.*

Guardian Angel: You were educated in England, were you not?

Nehru: Yes, I attended Harrow –

Guardian Angel: (*interrupts*) The same prep school as Mr. Churchill?

Nehru: Yes, though not at the same time. I then graduated from Cambridge and was later called to the Bar in London. So, there is much about the British that I admire. But the way they ruled India made a mockery of those ideals. Eventually it became clear that they did not want us as friends and colleagues, but as slaves to do their bidding. Underneath that civilized façade even the worst of them somehow project, the British exploited and extorted as ruthlessly as any other imperial power.

Guardian Angel: Please elaborate.

Nehru *nods and requests a sidebar.*

*A circle of four chairs materializes in the middle of the Courtroom.* Benjamin Franklin, John Adams, and Thomas Jefferson *appear and sit in three of them.*

Nehru *joins them and sits in the fourth.*

'Namaste,' gentlemen. I have long admired all of you, and it is indeed a pleasure to meet you.

Franklin: The pleasure is ours. We watched your Independence movement with great interest.

Adams: And cheered you on.

Jefferson: And were gratified to see you following our lead.

Nehru: The Declaration of Independence is an inspiration to all oppressed peoples. 'When in the course of human events, it becomes necessary to dissolve the political bonds'... But please, sir, would you continue?

Jefferson *smiles and nods.*
'We hold these truths to be self-evident, that all men are created equal, that they are endowed by their Creator with certain unalienable Rights, that among these are Life, Liberty and the pursuit of Happiness. That to secure these rights, Governments are instituted among Men, deriving their just powers from the consent of the governed. That whenever any Form of Government becomes destructive of these ends, it is the Right of the People to alter or to abolish it, and to institute new Government.'

R.A.Clio *hands* Nehru *a copy of the Declaration, which he scans carefully.*
It is difficult to get beyond all those ringing phrases of liberty. But moving down the page I come to the 'long train of abuses and usurpations.'

Hmmm... 'refused assent to laws'... 'forbidden to pass laws'... 'dissolved Representative Houses'... 'invasion of rights'... 'imposing taxes without consent'

Yes, we too were ruled from a far-away island and deprived of our right to govern ourselves. And also of our freedom of speech and the press. And for decades, they declared martial law when none was justified.

Adams: Fortunately, we were too far away for the British to effectively enforce most of their repressive laws. Mostly it was the precedent of things to come that alarmed us.

Nehru: We were even further away, but were cursed with an all-powerful foreign Viceroy with enough foreign troops to efficiently subjugate us.

Franklin: Most of our colonial governors were sufficiently incompetent to allow circumvention.

Nehru *returns to perusal of the 'abuses and usurpations'.*
Ah, now we're getting down to it: 'cutting off our Trade with all parts of the world.'

Franklin: Yes, we too were victims of the British Mercantile System.

Nehru: They exploited and drained us of our natural resources and required us to buy the finished products only from them. In the process, they destroyed native crafts and village industries. And then prevented our development of modern industry.

Adams: Amen, brother!

Nehru: You Americans were fortunate to escape the Empire early on, before all this exploitation impoverished your country. With us, they turned fertile and flourishing provinces into poverty-stricken dependencies. And their negligence and incompetence caused famine and pestilence. Meanwhile, they created a class of landlords who unjustly and mercilessly taxed the peasants.

<u>Jefferson:</u> That our colonies were on the edge of a vast frontier made that impractical with us. Besides, we had yeoman farmers instead of peasants.

<u>Nehru</u> *continues reading list...*'keeping among us, in times of peace, standing Armies without our Consent.'

<u>Adams:</u> Mostly of German mercenaries.

<u>Nehru:</u> Our situation was quite different. The British maintained a large army of occupation, composed primarily of Indian troops. BUT – *all* of the officers were *always* British. And the native soldiers themselves were never stationed in their native regions. Worst of all, the British used Indian regiments to subjugate and maintain other colonies in their Empire. Even when Japanese invasion was imminent, they stripped us of defense troops. All our best regiments were instead sent to fight elsewhere.

<u>Adams:</u> So they became like the hated Hessians!

<u>Nehru</u> *sighs and nods, then looks again at Declaration.*
But look here... 'to complete the works of death, desolation and tyranny, with cruelty and perfidy scarcely paralleled in the most barbarous ages'...

Oh come now, Gentlemen, with all due respect, isn't that a little much?

<u>Jefferson</u> *blushes and grins.* Well, perhaps my pen got a bit carried away.

<u>Nehru:</u> I certainly am not belittling the American struggle for Independence, but in terms of magnitude of suffering and longevity of resistance, it does not compare with ours.

Franklin: Again, we were lucky. How else to explain that 13 disunited, underequipped colonies were able to whip the mighty British Empire! Odds were that those of us signing that Declaration should have been hung as traitors.

Jefferson: It makes me nervous just thinking about it.

Adams: Not me. I knew America would eventually become an even greater Empire than the British.

Nehru: Which is perhaps why so many Americans don't understand that imperialism is truly evil. And the hypocrisy is even worse. Without our consent, they took us into a war for Freedom which they refused to give to us. They sabotaged our efforts to defend ourselves and threw our leaders in prison, where we were treated worse than German POWs. And meanwhile, they continued to encourage divisive issues and foment religious dispute. No one in the Moslem League was imprisoned; instead their idea of Pakistan was given credence. And so the eventual horror of religious warfare exploded after Partition.

Franklin: In general, the British were not kind to those with darker skin.

Nehru: They believed they were a race God destined to govern and subdue. They treated the great country of India as a chattel and contemptuously treated her people as an inferior race. They insisted that everything they did was just and noble, that it was *our* privilege to be ruled by them, and that we were the 'White Man's Burden.' They oppressed us unbearably – all the while claiming to civilize us.

Jefferson: Such racism is, alas, still present in our country. A sore that continues to fester. Perhaps we inherited that along with their Empire.

**Adams:** I hoped that our Empire would be better than theirs. But now I'm not so sure...

**Franklin:** In any case, I think we can all agree that India's experience as a British Colony was far worse than ours.

**Nehru:** And that being a 'Founding Father', so to speak, is never easy.

*Franklin, Jefferson, and Adams bid* Nehru *a cordial farewell and disappear. The chairs dematerialize.*

Nehru *returns to witness stand and indicates the disappearing chairs.*
Does that sort of thing happen often?

**Justice:** In Purgatory, only when necessary. Up – and down – there, such meetings happen all the time. Though of course, only with residents of one's own destiny.

Nehru *smiles and returns his attention to his testimony.*

**Guardian Angel:** And so you became involved in the Freedom Movement?

**Nehru:** Partly because of my father, who was one of the early leaders. And, of course, the influence of Gandhi was irresistible.

**Churchill:** Bah! Gandhi was a naked fakir in a loin cloth! His malevolent hair-splitting arguments and refusal to put up his fists encapsulated all that was repugnant about Hindus. He was the world's most successful humbug!

**Nehru:** *(with a flash of anger)* Who often went to jail for his principles of Nonviolent Resistance!

<u>Guardian Angel:</u> And how often did you?

<u>Nehru:</u> (*mentally counting up*) I was arrested and imprisoned 9 separate times. All together I spent at least 13 years – maybe more – in various British jails. But we all did. My entire family: father, mother, sisters, wife, aunts, nieces and nephews – and all the in-laws. Even my daughter, Indira, spent a year in prison when she was barely 18.

And British jails were NOT civilized. Not at all.

<u>Guardian Angel:</u> Given your previous lifestyle as Brahmins, this must have been a shock.

<u>Recording Angel</u> *opens her book to Anand Bhawan, a comfortable mansion of warm yellow stucco trimmed with cool blue wood, its two stories and rooftop porch surrounded by graceful railings and open verandas. A large cupola perches on top, crowned by an ornate onion dome. The many doors and windows, embroidered by lattice work, all add to the openness of the place. Spacious lawns and flowing fountains, copious flowers of all colors provide a perfect setting for a home that is generous and welcoming. Its many rooms are filled with family and friends and servants. Numerous books and various aspects of several civilizations decorate its shelves and walls. Above all, it is a joyous place, where laughter abounds. No one would <u>not</u> want to live there.*

*Viewing the occupants strolling the verandahs, one sees that all the women wear saris. The men, however, are dressed in custom-tailored western suits. But over time, the collars and cravats morph into sherwanis and dhoutis made of khadi. Gandhi and other leaders of the Freedom Movement are frequent guests. As always the conversation is stimulating, and an aura of vibrant purpose pervades.*

Nehru: My father was a <u>very</u> successful lawyer. *He shrugs rather sheepishly.* We even had an indoor swimming pool.

Guardian Angel: And you gave all this up?

Nehru: Yes. What the British didn't confiscate, we donated to the Freedom Movement.

Guardian Angel: Why did you sacrifice so much?

Nehru: Except for the imprisonment during the War – which was not of our choosing – we sacrificed gladly for our cause. But it took much patience – which wasn't always easy.

Recording Angel Clio *opens book to a railway station in India. It is the dead of night; there is no moon and clouds cover the stars. In the darkness, a train with windows shuttered stops at the siding. Soldiers emerge and stand at attention along the train. It is transporting a V.I.P. from one prison to a more secure one. His presence aboard is a secret, and yet thousands have gathered to cheer him. The crowd is peaceful, but shouts 'Jai Hind, Nehruji!' The British officer orders them to disperse. They refuse but make no effort to charge the line of additional guards descending from the train. They continue to cheer the prisoner. 'Jai Hind, Nehruji!' The guards begin to batter those in front with their iron-banded lathis. There are groans of pain as blood splatters, but no one backs down. Suddenly a man dressed in khadhi leaps out a window of the train, rushes the guards, and seizes the nearest lathi. He begins swinging it and yelling at the guards to stop beating the unarmed Indians. Obviously enraged, he knocks down several lathis and inflicts several wounds in the process. The guards rush to disarm him. The man continues to yell and swing. It takes at least six of them to finally subdue him. Some of them have bloody noses, as they drag the struggling prisoner back on the train. All the guards hastily reboard and the train leaves the station. The crowd follows it, still shouting 'Jai Hind, Nehruji!'*

<u>Nehru</u> *grins and shrugs, slightly embarrassed.*

<u>Devil's Advocate</u> *takes over, but with a much less aggressive manner than with Churchill.* Tell us about Partition.

<u>Nehru</u>: *(shaking his head sadly)* Dividing India made no sense. Geographically, we are a neatly demarcated area, cut off by the barrier of the Himalayas and surrounded by the Sea. As a whole, India is a self-sufficient unit. But divided, each part by itself is weak and dependent on others. And the division into India and Pakistan caused endless religious strife. At first I vehemently opposed it. But finally we consented to Partition because we thought that thereby we were purchasing peace and goodwill, though at a high price. Even now, if I had the same choice... But that decision should not have been forced on us! Even so, many of us hoped that Pakistan might eventually realize the folly of separation and rejoin India.

<u>Recording Angel</u>'s *book shows a mammoth human migration of mind-numbing dimension. Herds of human beings walk over open country past fires of villages burning all around them. The exhausted refugees are beyond wretched: covered with dust, feet bruised by stones, tortured by hunger and thirst, enrobed in a stench of urine, sweat and defecation. Strapped to backs are burdens surpassing a man's weight. On women's heads are balanced precarious piles of what they have been able to salvage from their homes. Emaciated horses pull anything with wheels or runners, on which are stacked hastily gathered belongings. The human debris left behind is ghastly. At every yard there is a dead body, some butchered, some dead of cholera. Vultures are so bloated they cannot fly. The stench is unbearable. And always they are stalked by the remorseless sun in a cloudless sky, from which the monsoon fails to come.*

*For hundreds of miles, these tragic columns trudge – in both directions. The Punjab has been divided. 5 million Hindus are leaving what is now Pakistan. On the other side, 5 million Muslims are leaving what is still India. The misery has compounded centuries of resentment; the upheaval has created bands of enraged men slaughtering each other. The new boundary line has also divided the territory of the Sikhs; they, too, are being displaced and getting caught in the crossfire. Many have joined the massacre.*

*The 'lucky' ones crowd trains in Lahore and Amritsar, clinging outside to the roof and sides like a swarm of bees. Often they are stopped in the countryside by marauding Muslims or Hindus or Sikhs. Everyone is mercilessly slaughtered with whatever is at hand. Many trains arriving at destinations are full of bloated butchered corpses, stinking and silent except for buzzing flies. Sometimes on the side is graffiti: 'A present from Pakistan', or 'A present from India.'*

<u>Nehru</u> *is overcome with grief, his head in his hands.*
No one saw this coming. Most of us didn't even believe Pakistan was coming. For centuries, Hindus and Muslims had lived together without excessive rancor. But clearly we underestimated the degree of Muslim resentment.

<u>Devil's Advocate:</u> And the appeal of a separate state?

<u>Nehru:</u> Yes, that too. And we really didn't take the Moslem League seriously. It was, after all, primarily a British creation – and lacked credible leadership.

<u>Devil's Advocate:</u> And then came Jinnah. You underestimated him, too?

<u>Nehru</u> *ponders.* No, I never underestimated Jinnah. He was as brilliant a lawyer as my father. They actually worked together in

the Congress party – even created a workable agreement between Hindus and Muslims.

Devil's Advocate: What happened to that?

Nehru: World War I! We all actively participated in it, thinking that our reward afterwards would be Dominion status.

Devil's Advocate: Which never happened?

Nehru: No! Instead the British inflicted numerous repressive decrees – which basically amounted to perpetual martial law. We felt betrayed and discouraged. The Freedom Movement waned.

Devil's Advocate: And then came Gandhi?

Nehru: Yes! Proclaiming Independence by means of nonviolence and civil disobedience. The older leaders of the Congress Party, bred in a more quiescent tradition, did not take easily to the new ways and were disturbed by the upsurge of the masses. Jinnah, especially, disliked crowds of ill-dressed people shouting in Hindi – and had no intention of ever going to prison. And khadi and sherwanis and dhoutis were definitely not his style. All his suits were custom-tailored in London, and he supposedly needed a special trunk just for all his shoes.

Devil's Advocate: And so he left India for London?

Nehru: For several years. And then, suddenly, he returned and emerged as the Leader the Moslem League had always lacked. Though we never doubted his ability, it was hard to take him seriously. He never practiced Islam – he ate pork, never went to mosque, didn't pray. And had nothing in common – and no respect for – the Muslims he somehow led. I don't think he even liked them. And he did not shed his western dress and monocle until the last possible moment. I truly do not understand what motivated Jinnah. Perhaps just the power to constantly say 'check' in a great game? *He shakes his head.*

Devil's Advocate: And he died shortly after Partition?

Nehru: Yes. Pakistan unfortunately remained.

Devil's Advocate: Tell the Court about Kashmir.

Nehru: *(with a look of far-away nostalgia)* Ah, Kashmir! The most beautiful place on Earth... My grandparents were from Kashmir.

Devil's Advocate: And this influenced your policy?

Nehru: I tried not to let it. But yes... Probably it did.

Devil's Advocate: Why the conflict there?

Nehru: It was on the border between India and Pakistan. The majority of Kashmiris were Muslim, so Pakistan invaded. The Hindu Maharajah asked India for help, so we sent troops.

Devil's Advocate: How did the U.N. get involved?

Nehru: We supported the United Nations and believed in its mission. So we referred the conflict to the U.N. for arbitration.

Devil's Advocate: And what was the result?

Nehru: After much debate, the U.N. decided that Kashmir should have a plebiscite to determine which country to join. Meanwhile, both sides were to withdraw their troops. We did. They didn't. And until the U.N. officials arrived, the Pakistani troops took more and more territory. How could there be a fair vote?

Devil's Advocate: What happened?

Nehru: Our troops went back in, and neither side could agree to solutions proposed by the U.N. mediators. *He sighs heavily.* And ever since it has been the main territory on which the continuing dispute between India and Pakistan has been played out. *He pauses, and sighs again.*

Devil's Advocate: Do you regret what you did?

Nehru: I was right to approach the U.N. for help; solving such disputes was, after all, why it was created. But I was naïve to believe that such a young organization was ready to handle something like this. And then, when the United States started sending weapons to Pakistan, it became a political football in the Cold War. And so ended all hope of re-unification.

Devil's Advocate: Why did the U.S. do that?

LBJ: (*standing up and angrily shaking his fist*) Because you guys were (**COLORFUL TEXAS PROFANITY**) Communists!

Justice: Mr. Johnson, please! You are out of order!

LBJ: I apologize, Your Honor, but they were!

Nehru: (*confronting LBJ*) No, Mr. President, we were not! We were Socialists! DEMOCRATIC Socialists! There's a huge difference!

LBJ: Then why were you and the Russians so cozy?

Nehru: Other than the railroads, the British left us with virtually no infra-structure on which to build our own heavy industry. We needed factories to make machines to make tools; we needed dams to provide energy to power them. And we needed them immediately. With our poverty-stricken masses, we could not afford the luxury of private enterprise. So the government did it by central command.

LBJ: And you let the Russians move in and take over!

Nehru: The Russians were generous in giving us machines and technicians to help us get started. They even brought their families, who lived alongside our technicians and their families. When the projects were finished, they returned to Russia and left behind lifelong friends in India. We shall always be grateful. And our nations, too, have always been good friends.

LBJ: Bah! They were just trying to get in your pants and make you go Communist!

Khrushchev: *(angrily)* No! Helping exploited peoples break free of colonialism was always a central policy of Communism. You Americans don't seem to understand what a terrible thing imperialism is.

Nehru: *(agreeing vigorously)* Despite British claims of benevolence, those parts of India which had been longest under their rule were the poorest. We were regarded as an excrescence, useful if we knew our place, otherwise a nuisance. And then came Gandhi: 'Get off the backs of these peasants and workers, all you who live by their exploitation. Get rid of this system that produces this poverty and misery.'

And this message was not just for India – but for all the other colonial countries and subject races. We were the acid test, the pre-eminent example of modern imperialism, the symbol of all colonial and exploited peoples. If India remained un-free, so would all those enslaved, and the War would have been fought in vain. And so when colonies all over the world followed our example and rose up for independence, they were glad to accept aid from the Russians.

Khrushchev: Why can't you (**EARTHY RUSSIAN PROFANITY**) imperialists understand something so obvious!

*Short* Khrushchev *and tall* LBJ *face off and trade heated invective.* Khrushchev *gets on a chair to literally get in* LBJ*'s face, who responds in kind. Much to* LBJ*'s surprise,* Khrushchev *resists the 'Johnson treatment.'*

Justice: Order! Order! Gentlemen, sit down!

De Gaulle, *who towers over both, breaks it up.* LBJ *and* Khrushchev *cool down and sit in opposite sides of jury box.*

Guardian Angel: Just for the record, were you a Communist?

Nehru: No. Never. We worked tirelessly for world disarmament, which we knew depended on removing the causes of war and national conflicts. This meant ending domination and exploitation by one group over another.

Khrushchev: *(popping up)* Yes, that's true. He was never a Communist. He should have been. But he was always a good neighbor nonetheless.

*A sharp glance from* Devil's Advocate *and he sits down again.*

Nehru, There was much that I admired about how the Soviet System successfully industrialized their country, but I was very aware of – and disapproved of – the repression that went with it. So yes, (*smiling at* <u>Khrushchev</u>) we were good neighbors. But I had no desire to join their camp. Or to join the other side. To embroil India in a war of giants would have been suicidal. But when elephants fight, the mice get trampled.

<u>Guardian Angel:</u> So you decided to organize the mice?

<u>Nehru:</u> That was the purpose of Non-alignment. Together we could provide a third option for developing countries. Lots of mice cooperating are a force to be reckoned with.

<u>Guardian Angel:</u> And it worked?

<u>Nehru:</u> For awhile. It gave us some breathing space to build India.

<u>Guardian Angel:</u> You were Prime Minister for 17 years. You could have easily become a Dictator – with the blessing of most of your people. Why didn't you?

<u>Nehru</u> *is taken aback, looks puzzled.* Why would I have done that? I never wanted power – I just wanted to make things better for my people.

*Back in the jury box, both* <u>LBJ</u> *and* <u>Khrushchev</u> *nod in agreement, then look at each other in surprise.*

<u>Nehru:</u> (*chuckling*) In fact, I often threatened to resign to get Parliament to behave. It usually worked because they knew I meant it.

<u>Guardian Angel:</u> As leader of the Non-aligned countries, you often mediated between East and West?

Nehru: Yes, I did. For example, I knew Ho Chi Minh quite well, and served as a communication link between him and the French. And several Arab countries were part of our group, so I was sometimes able to cool things down in the Middle East.

Guardian Angel: *(treading gently)* And for awhile, China was a part of this group?

Nehru *sighs heavily and looks down. After a long pause, he speaks quietly.* Yes, that's true. We shared a long border, had rich ancient traditions, and had achieved Independence about the same time. We were natural allies! I greatly admired Chinese culture. And...

Guardian Angel: *(prompting gently)* And Zhou En Lai?

Nehru: Yes, I admired him too. We had so much in common, and could converse about everything. He, too, was well-educated; he, too, had suffered much to free his country. I always looked forward to our meetings.

Guardian Angel: He was a good friend?

Nehru: Yes! And he was the brother I'd always wanted.

Guardian Angel: So what happened?

Nehru: Suddenly Chinese troops attacked our border in the Himalayas.

Guardian Angel: You were surprised?

Nehru: I was shocked... Though I shouldn't have been. It was a border dispute of long standing. And my Generals had repeatedly warned me and urged us to prepare.

Guardian Angel: Why didn't you?

Nehru: Our army was already fighting on the Pakistan border. I didn't think we could handle war on two fronts... And I trusted Zhou En Lai when he said it would never happen. We had done so much to help China's Communist Government gain legitimacy in the eyes of the world. I could not believe he would betray us... betray me.

Guardian Angel: And when it happened?

Nehru: I had not prepared for what my Army leaders knew was coming. The Chinese Army was five times the size of ours – and had all the latest Soviet weapons. Our army was trained for tank warfare in the desert – not fighting in the mountains. And it was woefully underequipped. Everything possible went wrong. It was a disaster.

*He bows his head and is silent.*

*Finally he speaks.*
We were defeated. Decisively. And it was my fault. I should have known and been ready. But I trusted Zhou... *The pain in his voice is etched on his face.*

Guardian Angel *gently pats his hand.*

*A very long pause*

Justice: *(voice unsteady, speaks quietly)* You are dismissed.

Nehru: Yes, I should have been. I died instead.

*Shoulders slumped, unsmiling, head down, he walks slowly back to jury box. He sits between LBJ and Khrushchev, who give him sympathetic looks, and move closer on either side of him.*

## CHAPTER 5

# KHRUSHCHEV (1894 – 1971)

Justice: The Court calls Nikita Khrushchev, 1st Secretary of the Communist Party and Premier of the Soviet Union, to the Witness Stand.

Khrushchev: *bounces good-naturally to the Chair and sits down.*

Guardian Angel: Mr. Khrushchev –

Khrushchev *interrupts with friendly smile.* Comrade Khrushchev, if you please.

Guardian Angel: Comrade Khrushchev, you come from humble origins, yes?

Khrushchev: *(proudly)* My father was a miner, and we were very poor. Most of us couldn't even read.

Guardian Angel: So how did you end up Leader of the powerful Soviet Union?

Khrushchev: It was the Revolution that made it possible. Without that – and The Party – people like me would have remained oppressed by the bourgeoisie.

Guardian Angel: This was a very turbulent time in your country's history, was it not?

Khrushchev: (shrugs) This is how things change in Russia. Much chaos and bloodshed. But this time the people won!

Recording Angel's *screen fast-forwards the major events of the Russian Revolution. First one sees the peasants of Russia, drafted into the Tsar's army to fight Germany and Austria in World War I. They have no idea why. Poorly dressed and mostly unarmed, they are ordered into battle, with instructions to scavenge weapons from dead comrades on the battlefield. There is not enough to eat and their wounds are rarely tended, but the Russian soldiers fight bravely and charge enemy lines over and over. Millions die.*

*Finally, they throw their bayonets into the earth and start walking home. Meanwhile in the Capitol, there is a bloodless revolution. The Tsar abdicates, and Alexander Kerensky declares a constitutional republic. But he continues the War. The military disaster continues, and on the homefront people are starving. Millions die.*

*The Germans send exiled Lenin back to Russia. After another bloodless coup, the Bolsheviks depose Kerensky and take over. Lenin makes Peace with Germany at the cost of Russia's buffer zones. Russia's former allies send troops to help restore the Tsar and bring Russia back into the War. A bloody Civil War erupts as Whites and Reds fight all over the country. Meanwhile the peasants dispose of their landlords, and defend themselves from all sides. Millions die.*

*Trotsky organizes the Red Army and sends armoured trains to defeat opposition all around. The Tsar is executed, the foreign troops leave, the Whites are defeated, and the peasant rebellions put down. Millions die.*

*The victorious Bolsheviks try to rebuild a huge – and totally ravaged – Russia. Famine and pestilence stalk the land as they endeavor to make order out of chaos. Millions die.*

*The Communist Party is now in power and has inherited a seemingly hopeless task.*

Khrushchev: Russia was devastated. The Party took command and we worked long and hard – and gladly – to rebuild on all the rubble. Education was a priority of the new government, and I grasped whatever opportunities were available. Even so, most of us were primarily self-educated. After years of devoted labor, working day and night – or so it seemed – I rose in the ranks of The Party.

Recording Angel's *screen must pan out – again and again – to get a complete view of Russia. It occupies all of northern Asia. On the west is a piece of Europe. The northern border rims the Arctic Circle. On each end it has only one warm-water port: Leningrad in the West and Vladivostok in the East. The far North latitude of the huge land mass in between results in rigorous climate; much of it is covered with permafrost several feet thick. Underneath is a wealth of natural resources capable of making Russia self-sufficient – if only one can get at them. Such a place requires strong, hardy people who know how to endure.*

*Moving in closer, the screen goes slowly from West to East. It takes a long time to pass through all eleven time zones. The cities in the West become only a few once past the Urals. All of them are insignificant compared to the vast steppe and forest which constantly threaten to engulf them.*

At first, one sees that much of this human imprint has been wrecked. Then groups of people appear, fixing what was broken and building much more. Factories and dams are laboriously constructed in the middle of nowhere; blocks of shoddy apartment buildings are hastily erected nearby. Palaces are repaired and turned into museums; concert halls are renovated for musicians and dancers who have somehow kept their art alive. And schools are everywhere, trying to educate a nation of illiterates.

Though modern technology could obviously be of great assistance in this monumental task, not much is in evidence. The West rarely sells to Russia, because they will not take rubles in exchange – and because their governments refuse diplomatic recognition to the new Communist regime. So most of the labor is done the hard way, by people of all ages and genders. In the less inhospitable areas, the long hours are borne in a spirit of hope for the new world they are building. In the wilds of Siberia, where the climate is nearly impossible, most of the labor is done by convicts in the Gulag. There is not enough to go around for anyone; the prisoners get less than the volunteers.

As time passes, one sees that Russia is being industrialized. Steel mills are producing tractors and tanks, dams are generating energy to power them. Life is slowly improving for the people; everyone still works long hours, but most have learned to read. In Siberia, however, the size of the Gulag increases.

Then another War breaks out. The Germans invade again and destroy most of what has been so laboriously built by the Russian people. Millions – and millions – die.

As the screen passes over Russia, one sees again massive devastation. Déjà vu. The Russians endure and rebuild once again. But this time their borders are much farther to the West, including many East

*European countries as buffer zones. And the factories start producing missiles and nuclear submarines.*

*They will never let all this happen again. No matter what.*

*As the screen fades, there is profound silence. Everyone in the courtroom is stunned by all the monumental tragedy R.A.Clio has shown them. Only Khrushchev is not surprised. But even he sits silently with bowed head.*

*Finally the Devil's Advocate approaches and gently resumes her cross-examination.*
You eventually became one of Stalin's protégés?

*Khrushchev rouses from his memories and answers.*
Yes. And was proud to be so. You must understand what a huge country Russia is, and how great the destruction was, and how much needed to be done – and how quickly it had to be done to catch up. There had to be a strong leader to guide The Party and make it happen.

Devil's Advocate: You then became Boss of the Ukraine?

Khrushchev: I became First Secretary of the Communist Party of the Ukraine. Later, when the War started, I became its Commissar as well. Stalin sent me there to restore order. That meant arresting people. The entire upper echelon of leading officials, several layers deep, was destroyed. Sometimes even their replacements were arrested and shot, too.

Devil's Advocate: So at Stalin's orders, you sentenced thousands to death and to the Gulag. Why?

Khruschev: Ukraine was our breadbasket, and was not producing enough food to feed our hungry people. We organized

Collective Farms and tried various other means, but the peasants did not cooperate. Our factories were more productive, but there, too, we had problems with shirkers. Eventually we had to view them all as traitors. The Party said so, and we had to protect The Party.

Devil's Advocate: So these people deserved to die?

Khrushchev: Some of them, yes. They were Saboteurs, Enemies of the People left over from the Civil War. And we were surrounded by a world out to get us.

Devil's Advocate: Aren't you being paranoid?

Khrushchev:: To fear an actual menace is to be realistic – not paranoid. Just look at the map!

Recording Angel *opens her book to a map of the world from the top down. Viewed from the North Pole, one sees that Russia is indeed encircled by the U.S. and its allies. In all these countries are U.S. army bases and/or missile installations – all aimed at the USSR.*

Khrushchev *is fascinated by* R.A.Clio's *'book', and wanders over to the screen, trying to figure out how it works.*

Devil's Advocate *recalls him to the witness stand and returns his attention to the issue at hand.* But surely there were some who were innocent?

Khrushchev: *(sadly)* In retrospect, yes there were. Many comrades I knew well were denounced. I was often surprised. Someone I liked and thought was an honest fellow and a good Communist would be called a traitor. Then I felt tormented. Had I been a fool to trust him? Must I do as I was told and arrest him? *Shakes his head.* Sometimes I took sin upon my soul, in the interests of the Party.

But back then, we thought Stalin was God, and that he saw things we were blind to. His actions were seen as decisiveness, of his unbending will in defense of the Soviet state, to strengthen it against its enemies, whoever they might turn out to be. And some of his bootlickers would have cut their own father's throat if Stalin had merely blinked.

Devil's Advocate: Did that attitude change when you eventually joined Stalin's inner circle?

Khrushchev: Not at first. But after the War, we would be summoned to his private quarters for gargantuan feasts and marathon drinking bouts. Stalin usually stayed sober – and in control – but insisted all of us get drunk. Really drunk. After awhile, it undermined my health.

Devil's Advocate: So were you relieved at his death?

Khrushchev: Personally, yes. But there was genuine grief among the people. He had been God for almost 30 years. Even those of us who knew better felt uncertain about the future.

Devil's Advocate: I would imagine there was quite a power struggle.

Khrushchev: Yes – in typical Russian fashion. I behaved no better – or worse – than the others. But that just goes with the territory of our history.

Devil's Advocate: And you won. Even though you weren't considered a frontrunner for the top job. How did you manage that?

<u>Khrushchev:</u> No comment. *He shrugs.*

<u>Guardian Angel</u> *takes over his interrogation.* One of your first acts in power was to denounce Stalin. Why?

*The lights dim, with a spotlight on* <u>Khrushchev</u>. *It widens to a circle of Central Committee members who are the top leadership of The Party. The report of a recent commission has disclosed all the false arrests and executions during the Purges. They are discussing what report of this should be given to the Twentieth Party Congress – the first to meet since Stalin's death.*

<u>Khrushchev:</u> Comrades, what are we going to do about this?

<u>Others:</u> We can just keep blaming Beria.

<u>Khrushchev:</u> (*sarcastically*) So it was not God who was to blame, but the lower ranking 'saints'? They didn't report accurately, so God sent down thunder and lightning? People suffered not because God wanted them to, but because the Prophet Beria was bad?
But you can't keep washing a black cat till it turns white! And Stalin was the Black Cat!

<u>Others:</u> But why tell the Congress that? Better to sweep it under the rug.

<u>Khrushchev:</u> But many innocent people will soon be returning from exile. We must figure out how to bring them back.

<u>Others:</u> Why must they come back?

<u>Khrushchev:</u> Their sentences are over. We can't keep them any longer. And we certainly can't execute them, as Beria proposed. We must exonerate them.

<u>Others:</u> What's the matter with you?! You think you can tell this to the Congress? They'll point at us. What can we say about our own role?

<u>Khrushchev:</u> But the Congress will soon disperse. Released prisoners will be coming back and telling relatives and friends what happened. Then the Delegates – and the whole Party – will say 'But excuse me, what's going on here? Nobody said anything at the Congress. How could you leaders not have known what was going on?

<u>Others:</u> We'll be called to account! We were part of the leadership, and if we didn't know the whole truth, so much the worse for us. But we'll be held responsible for it all.

<u>Khrushchev:</u> But we didn't have the right <u>not</u> to know. Some of us were unaware of many things, since you were supposed to know only what you were told. You weren't supposed to stick your nose into anything else. And we didn't.

<u>Others:</u> But don't you see what will happen?

<u>Khrushchev:</u> I am prepared to bear my share of the responsibility, if the Party sees fit to so blame those who were with Stalin when this tyranny held sway.

<u>Others</u> *disagree and object. But they are unable to unite against him. Their fear of one another is too great.*

*The next day,* <u>Khrushchev</u> *addresses the Assembled Delegates. There are dark circles under his eyes. There is absolute silence. One can hear the buzz of a fly.*

*It is supposed to be a Secret. But soon everyone in the World knows about Stalin's crimes.* <u>Khrushchev</u> *and the* Others *are not punished, because for everyone in the Gulag, there are several others who had denounced them. Culpability for the Purges multiplies and extends outward in concentric circles, to the many who had betrayed friends to save themselves.*

*And thus begins a very painful reconciliation among the Russian People.*

Guardian Angel: Any regrets?

Khrushchev *shakes head.* No. It was the right thing to do. And it had to be done.

Devil's Advocate: But you still approved of Stalin's actions in Eastern Europe?

Khrushchev: Of course! Russia has no natural boundaries, so someone is always trying to invade us.

Devil's Advocate: Like the Germans?

Khrushchev: Twice in my lifetime! So we need buffer states to defend ourselves.

Devil's Advocate: So you weren't trying to take over all of Europe?

Khrushchev: How could we? Our country was totally devastated!

Devil's Advocate: What about Berlin?

Khrushchev *snorts and shakes his head.* Dividing it between East and West, and sticking it right in the middle of East Germany – that was a crisis just waiting to happen! What were they thinking at the Potsdam Conference?!

Churchill: That wasn't my fault!

Justice: Do you have something to say, Sir Winston?

Churchill: I would, if my ungrateful country hadn't thrown me out of office! The new Prime Minister hadn't a clue about what was going on!

LBJ: Neither did our new President. Truman was a good man – but he was no Roosevelt.

Khrushchev: And neither of them was a match for Stalin! He negotiated with great skill and defended Russia from the West.

Devil's Advocate: Better than he defended Russia from himself?

Khrushchev *opens mouth, then closes it and is silent. Finally:*
But getting back to Berlin, the Wall was Walter Ulbricht's idea. He was the real Boss of East Germany. When we finally gave his East Germans the OK, we had no idea they would build it virtually overnight.

Oh, those efficient Germans! It would have taken us months – maybe even years.

Devil's Advocate: Tell us about the Missile Race.

Khrushchev: Our people were exhausted. For decades they had labored and fought and done without just about everything. It was time to stop making tanks and start giving our people decent housing – and what goes with it. But we could never afford guns and butter. And how could we send our huge armies home with the United States and its allies constantly threatening our boundaries?

Devil's Advocate: So you decided to build nuclear missiles.

Khrushchev: Yes! Much cheaper than standing armies. They would deter attack and let us divert our resources to consumer goods.

Devil's Advocate: So Russia started the Nuclear Arms Race?

Khrushchev: That's not how it was supposed to work out. We had very few missiles actually off the drawing board. But I bluffed that we were turning out missiles like sausages.

Devil's Advocate: And the U.S. believed you?

Khrushchev: Yes! But then they started sending high altitude surveillance planes over our territory.

Devil's Advocate: Planes that were looking for missile installations? Which didn't yet exist?

Khrushchev: Exactly. So I met with President Eisenhower. He knew what I was up to, and knew why. He was a General, and had visited Russia immediately after the Armistice. He saw all the ruins firsthand.

But unlike Russia, America could afford guns and butter. Even so, Ike worried about the power of his own Military Industrial Complex.

Devil's Advocate: So he called off the U-2 flights?

Khrushchev: Yes! And we planned a Summit Meeting in Paris to start disarmament of all our military forces.

Devil's Advocate: What happened?

Khrushchev: The CIA insisted on just one more U-2 flight. This one we were finally able to shoot down! And the pilot didn't self-destruct, as ordered.

Devil's Advocate: And the Summit?

Khrushchev: It was a disaster. Ike betrayed me. How could I trust him?

Devil's Advocate: Without the U-2 incident, could the Cold War have stopped right then?

Khrushchev: *(tears running down his cheeks)* Yes. Both of us were ready, both of us had enough power to convince our generals... Think of all the suffering that wouldn't have happened. *He can't speak through his grief.*

Justice: The Court is recessed until tomorrow.

*Fade out.*

*The next day, the Court reconvenes.*

Devil's Advocate: Why did you send Nuclear Missiles to Cuba?

Khrushchev: Cuba had just broken free from imperialism – and then was invaded by the U.S. Castro was our friend and ally. We had to help him build Cuba – just as we had helped India.

Devil's Advocate: But you didn't give Nehru missiles.

Khrushchev: We didn't need to – India isn't 90 miles from Florida!

LBJ: Which is why we couldn't have a Communist on our doorstep!

Khrushchev: Castro wasn't a Communist – at first. You pushed him into our camp. And we welcomed him with open arms. Our own Revolution was so distant – the blood of idealism no longer pulsed in our veins. And here was this young hero, who had liberated his country right under the nose of the most powerful Imperialist. How could we not help him! How could we not defend this small country giving the finger to the Giant of Capitalism!

LBJ: But surely you knew we couldn't let you get away with it!

Khrushchev: But we almost did! The idea was to install the missiles secretly and present the U.S. with a *fait accompli*. And our technicians moved almost as fast as the East Germans did in Berlin.

Devil's Advocate: What happened?

Khrushchev: Those (**FURIOUS RUSSIAN PROFANITY**) U-2 planes finally recognized what was going on. And thus commenced the so-called Cuban Missile Crisis. The nuclear warheads were already en route when the U.S. blockade was deployed.

Devil's Advocate: How close did my Boss come to winning?

Khrushchev: Much too close. Fortunately, President Kennedy was able to resist his Generals. We worked out a deal: We'll send our missiles home, if you promise not to invade Cuba. And get your missiles out of Turkey. And yes, we'll keep this secret so you can save face. The U.S. claimed the Missile Crisis as a Victory.

My generals saw it that way, too. And those in the higher ranks of The Party started maneuvering.

Guardian Angel: Were you responsible for Kennedy's assassination?

Khrushchev: Absolutely not! During the Crisis, he and I discovered we could work together to keep Peace. That's when the hotline was installed. So I was shocked – and saddened. Such a fine young man. I sent a sympathy letter to his widow. So did my wife.

Guardian Angel: And eventually you were deposed.

Khrushchev: And allowed to live. Which didn't usually happen in my country.

Guardian Angel: How generous!

Khrushchev: Not really. I was confined to my dacha – not luxurious but adequate. But I was a virtual prisoner and cut off from everything. I was not allowed to contribute to my country all that I had learned about the world. I saw all my accomplishments undone by my successors. People stopped visiting – and I was written out of my own country's history.

Guardian Angel: And what happened to Soviet-American relations?

Khrushchev: They got worse. And the arms race escalated to obscene proportions. With me it had been a deterrent, a bluff. But the U.S. took it seriously. And every time they escalated, so did Brezhnev. All I could do was watch.

*He deflates and sits silently.*

Justice: (*finally*) You are dismissed.

Khrushchev: Yes, I was. But they let me live. A legacy that lasted.

*He brightens a bit at the thought, returns to jury box and sits next to* Nehru, *who pats his shoulder sympathetically.* LBJ *looks thoughtful.*

# CHAPTER 6

# DE GAULLE (1890-1970)

Justice: The Court calls General Charles De Gaulle, President of France.

*De Gaulle approaches the Bench and faces* Justice, *standing at attention.*

Justice: At ease, Monsieur le General. Take the witness stand, s'il vous plait.

De Gaulle: Merci, Madame de Justice.

Guardian Angel: Bonjour, Monsieur le General.

De Gaulle: *(sitting with straight back, as if he'd swallowed an extra long yardstick)* Bonjour, Madame.

Guardian Angel: Thanks to Clio, I was able to scan your obituaries. One of them simply said, 'De Gaulle is dead. France is a widow.'

De Gaulle: (*nodding sadly*) France has always been the Love of My Life. My father was a History teacher at a Jesuit school, and from him I learned of her *gloire*. And also of the times when the French were not worthy of her. *He frowns and pauses.* We were encouraged to discuss these matters at the family dinner table – Jesuit style, of course – and I often organized the neighborhood children in re-enactments of important battles. *He smiles – almost – remembering.* When I was eleven, we moved to Paris. That's when I really fell in love. In the most beautiful of cities, how could I not?! And so I resolved to dedicate my life to protecting France.

Guardian Angel: And you eventually attended the St. Cyr Military Academy, where the elite Army officers are trained, n'est-ce pas?

De Gaulle: Oui, c'est vrai.

Guardian Angel: You graduated near the top of the class and fought with exceptional valor in the First Great War. Afterward, however, you were repeatedly passed over for promotion. Why?

De Gaulle: My beloved France was totally ravished during that War. I <u>had</u> to make sure it never happened again. Malheureusement, my ideas collided with the false sense of security created by the Maginot Line. Terrified of another war, French leaders – military and otherwise – would not listen to what they needed to hear.

Guardian Angel: And I see that during the Second World War, you often irritated the Allied leaders with what they considered arrogance and lack of political realism.

De Gaulle: No, it was not arrogance – nor lack of political understanding. I <u>knew</u> they considered France of <u>no</u> importance.

But they were wrong! Even though the <u>French</u> Army had stopped fighting, and the <u>French</u> politicians were collaborating, FRANCE was still the great power she had been for centuries! And I insisted that she be treated accordingly.

<u>Guardian Angel:</u> And as a result, France was given a zone of occupation in Germany, n'est-ce pas?

<u>De Gaulle:</u> Even though decisions were made affecting our vital interests, France was not invited to the conferences at Yalta and Potsdam. But Churchill thought the Americans would soon go home. And that the Russians would stay. So he insisted that France also be an occupying power.

<u>Guardian Angel:</u> Who decided that you should lead France after the War?

<u>De Gaulle:</u> The French people. When France is in great trouble, her people often turn to a strong leader who can make order out of chaos – figuratively speaking, a 'man-on-horseback'. Though I had no horse when I led the Victory Parade in Paris, I assumed the role with traditional valor.

<u>Recording Angel</u> *shows a huge crowd gathered along the Champs-Élysées. They are eager, but rather subdued for Parisians. Life under the Nazis has been grim; only collaborators have had enough – almost – of anything. There is, however, a sense of quiet relief that the departing Germans did not follow Hitler's orders to torch Paris. A band begins playing 'La Marseillaise'. Weary backs straighten, bowed heads are lifted, a whisper of pride becomes an audible cry. And then, under Napoleon's Arc de Triumph, appears the very tall* <u>French</u> *General, leading the battle-tested* <u>French</u> *troops who have liberated Paris. Waving tri-color flags appear everywhere as Parisians ecstatically shout 'Vive la France! Vive De Gaulle!' Many are weeping, but this time with joy – not shame.*

*As De Gaulle marches alone, ahead of his troops, shots ring out. Lingering German snipers are everywhere, and De Gaulle is a perfect target. But the general does not flinch, does not miss a beat, his military bearing does not falter. As he triumphantly salutes the sea of tri-colors, the crowd roars proudly 'Vive De Gaulle!'*

*Later he speaks from the balcony of the Hotel de Ville to the jubilant crowd below:*

Paris outraged, Paris broken, Paris martyred, but Paris liberated! And soon, all of France. She is a great world power! She has a right to be heard, and will act so that others may know it. *Tricolor flags wave, as the French joyously sing 'La Marseillaise', so long forbidden.*

Guardian Angel: But at the time, there must have been a lot to do in France first.

De Gaulle: Mais oui! Much housing had been destroyed, basic public services were at a standstill, petrol and electricity were scarce, and there was very little food. The main problem was that transport was virtually paralyzed. Most railroad tracks had been bombed, modern equipment and rolling stock taken to Germany, and many bridges destroyed.

Guardian Angel: How did you deal with all that?

De Gaulle: I nationalized energy companies and major banks and anything else conceivably in the public domain, as well as several important private enterprises which had collaborated and made huge profits under the Nazis.

Guardian Angel: And collaborators in general?

De Gaulle: In France, they were more severely punished than in other occupied countries. The Resistance Partisans were especially vengeful – understandably so. But I knew that it was important to get this process under firm judicial control. Although it was certainly necessary to punish traitors, I also knew that those who had played minor roles under Vichy – police, civil servants, and such – had to be reprieved to keep the country running as normally as possible. As head of state, I assumed the right to commute death sentences. Out of 2000+ so convicted, less than 800 were actually executed. But I refused to pardon those whose role in the murder of Jews was even worse than treason.

Guardian Angel: And what happened to members of the Resistance?

De Gaulle: That was difficult. As much as I valued their courage under the Occupation, I knew that the most effective among them were Communists. And after the war, they became the largest political party. Although I could not dispute their participation in the government, I was unwilling to trust a party I considered an agent of a foreign power. So I did not grant them any important Cabinet ministries. They were not pleased. But after all, I was the man-on-horseback, so...

Guardian Angel: And did you enjoy being 'on horseback'?

De Gaulle: Not really. Despite my reputation for arrogance, I am basically rather shy, and disliked the personal aspects of politics. I was not good in social situations, or at public speaking. But I knew I needed to rally the nation to the new government. So I went on tour.

Guardian Angel: Recording Angel Clio tells me you often disregarded your own safety by mixing with the crowds and making yourself an easy target for assassins – of whom there were still many about.

De Gaulle: Yes, well – anywhere I was always the tallest, so what did it matter? *He shrugs.* I was not a very good orator, but by using amplification and patriotic music, I was able to convey my message that though all of France was fragmented and suffering, together we would rise again. Halfway through I would invite the crowd to join me in 'La Marseillaise'. And when I finished my speech, I would raise my hands *(which he does)* and cry, 'Vive la France!' *(With great fervor.)*

Guardian Angel: But despite all this, only 2 months after forming the new government, you resigned. Why?

De Gaulle: Liberté, Égalité, Fraternité are all very well in theory, but in practice – especially in France – they often result in parliamentary anarchy. *He sighs.* For decades, ministerial Cabinets had come tumbling down with appalling frequency. It is impossible to have a strong nation with so much unstable government. *He sighs again.* And sure enough, soon after I had restored order out of the worst of the postwar chaos, the various political parties began squabbling. *He shakes his head.* How can one govern a country which has 246 varieties of cheese! *A wry grin.* I knew I could not give France the leadership she deserved under such circumstances. So I warned the French: 'Let me do the job properly. Or I will resign.'

Guardian Angel: And then?

De Gaulle: They let me resign. I went home and waited for the French to recall me.

Guardian Angel: Which took 12 years. What did you do in between?

De Gaulle: I wrote my Memoirs. And kept in touch with former lieutenants, who helped me remain the best informed person in France.

Guardian Angel: And what did you observe?

De Gaulle: Despite recurring Cabinet crises, France began to recover economically. But her foreign policy was one disaster after another. After the debacle in IndoChina, especially, it became apparent that the French colonial empire was an anachronistic burden. Shortly after I returned to power, I offered all the colonies a choice of immediate independence or of joining the new French Community. Most of them elected to join what was our version of the British Commonwealth.

Churchill: You make it sound so easy!

De Gaulle: Au contraire! For a man of my age and upbringing, it was bitterly cruel to become the overseer of such a transformation. Our country had put forth immense effort to develop her overseas dependencies. But the maintenance of our authority over countries no longer willing to accept it was becoming a hazard from which we had everything to lose and nothing to gain. What an agonizing ordeal to hand over power, furl our flags, and close a great chapter of our History!

Guardian Angel: And Algeria?

De Gaulle: Algeria was a special case. It was technically part of France itself, and to many French settlers it had been home for several generations. For them, Independence would mean being governed by the Arab majority and a reversal of decades of privilege. A bloody Civil War erupted, with many Algerian Army officers forming the Organisation de l'Armée Secrète opposing Independence. Terror crossed the Mediterranean and wreaked havoc even in France itself. I myself was the object of several assassination attempts. When Algerian Independence was at last declared, a million dispossessed and embittered French settlers returned to France.

*In Algiers, OAS terrorists with sub-machine guns roar through the streets exterminating Moslems, who reciprocate amidst blood-curdling yells. Thousands are slaughtered, atrocities abound on both sides. Frightened French settlers plan to return to France. They are executed as traitors and property left behind is destroyed. 'Let us leave it as we found it.' Schools, town halls, factories, shops and offices are systematically burned down all over the country. In Algiers, the University goes up in flames. Meanwhile, terrified French Algerians mob the harbor, desperate for passage to Marseilles. Bombs explode all over metropolitan France. En route to the Paris airport, De Gaulle's car is ambushed by a hail of bullets at point-blank range, then pursued by a carload of gunmen. At least 150 bullets are fired at De Gaulle, who emerges unscathed – and undeterred.*

Devil's Advocate *takes over questioning.* You were recalled primarily because of the Algerian crisis, and having emergency powers was a condition of your return, n'est-ce pas?

De Gaulle: How else could I be an effective 'man-on-horseback'?

Devil's Advocate: And when Algerian Independence was finally achieved?

De Gaulle: I proposed a constitutional amendment for the President to have more power and be directly elected by universal suffrage.

Devil's Advocate: How did this go over with the National Assembly?

De Gaulle: They accused me of wanting to be a dictator. *Scoffs.* Who honestly believes that at age 67, I would start a career as a dictator?

Devil's Advocate: Hmmm. And your reaction?

De Gaulle: I dissolved the National Assembly.

Devil's Advocate: *(sarcastically)* Not a dictator, eh?

De Gaulle: *(offended)* Of course not! I made it clear to the French that I would lead as long as they followed. And when they stopped, I resigned. Just as I promised I would.

Devil's Advocate: Eleven years later, I see. Recording Angel Clio tells me those were years of prosperity for the French. Which gave you time to make France a world power again.

De Gaulle: France did not need an Empire to be great. My vision was for her to be a Third Force moderating the hostility between the two superpowers.

Devil's Advocate: Like at the 1960 Paris Summit?

De Gaulle: Ah, what an opportunity that was! And could have been! The Cold War might have ended right then and there!

Devil's Advocate: How so?

De Gaulle: Both sides were ready. Both leaders were decent, responsible men who had made a connection that could have developed into a real working partnership. I myself knew and respected both Eisenhower and Khrushchev. I understood where each was coming from, had cordial relations with both, and invited them to Paris to help them start winding down the arms race.

Devil's Advocate: What happened?

De Gaulle: That accursed U-2 plane got shot down! Both men were genuinely dismayed – but handled the situation badly. Despite my best efforts to mediate, the Summit collapsed.

Devil's Advocate: With great loss of face for you.

De Gaulle: *(angrily)* That was never the point! And besides, everyone praised my attempts to mediate. What mattered was that a window of opportunity had opened to end the insanity of the Cold War. Instead it slammed shut and the arms race escalated to even more obscene proportions.

Devil's Advocate: And then you made France a player, too. Didn't another country with The Bomb make things worse?

De Gaulle *is silent, thinking.* Point taken. But being a nuclear power was the only way to get a place at the high stakes table of diplomacy. But though the USA had helped England develop their Bomb, Secretary of State Dulles warned that American missiles would be aimed at France if we tried to get one of our own. *He snorts.* When our tests were successful, I announced that the French nuclear force would be capable of firing in all directions.

Devil's Advocate: Oh, now *(shakes her head)*, would you really have done that?

De Gaulle: *(a bit embarrassed)* No, of course not. For us, The Bomb really was only a deterrent. But someone from the West had to stand up to the Americans! They were so self-righteous! And so ignorant of what it meant to be a world leader.

LBJ: We knew enough to bail you guys out – twice! If you Europeans weren't always squabbling, we wouldn't need to get involved. *His face reddens as he suppresses colorful Texas profanity rendered inappropriate by* De Gaulle's *imposing persona.*

Devil's Advocate: And the Russians?

De Gaulle: The Russians had been around long enough to know that realistic foreign policy was based on comprehending everyone's self-interest as well as one's own. What Stalin did after the War, for example, was what Peter the Great would have done. But the Americans didn't understand this, and thought their self-interest was – or ought to be – that of the whole world. With all their wealth and power, they were a veritable menace. And they always thought they were the good guys. No matter what.

LBJ: But we are the good guys!

Guardian Angel *interjects, shaking her head.* My Boss finds that intensely annoying. Especially when you Americans insist that God is always on your side. *Shakes her head again.* You're even worse than the British.

De Gaulle: *(nodding)* Indeed. Which is why I withdrew the French Mediterranean fleet from NATO, and refused to participate in any more NATO maneuvers. I also took France out of SEATO, and told the U.S. to remove all their nuclear weapons and military personnel from French territory.

Devil's Advocate: Doubtless they were vexed.

De Gaulle: Ah yes, their Secretary of State asked if this included exhumation of the American war dead buried in French cemeteries. One hopes he was indulging in sarcasm.

Devil's Advocate: And you had some more surprises up your sleeve. My boss has always enjoyed your unpredictability.

De Gaulle: As a lifelong Catholic, knowing that does not please me. *He scowls.* However, the Americans had insisted that West Germany be part of NATO – which was part of our problem with the organization as a whole. But much to everyone's surprise, I made an end run and initiated rapprochement with the Germans.

Devil's Advocate: Even my boss was shocked! The Germans had invaded France twice in your lifetime. And again shortly before. And always with great devastation. How could you possibly be allies?

Khrushchev *waves his fist.*

De Gaulle: For centuries, we had been at war with the British. And yet we allied with them for World Wars I and II. Germany had been a united country for less than <u>one</u> century. And its driving force was Prussia, which was now in East Germany. So it was possible – and made much sense – to connect with our next-door neighbor. Chancellor Adenauer and I had much in common in our European outlook. And we were both devout Catholics. And it helped that my German was much better than my English. We became personal friends, as well as leaders of the drive toward European unity.

Devil's Advocate: Had Adenauer been a Nazi?

De Gaulle: No, he was wisely of no consequence in the Third Reich. And even spent time in prison. Though not one of the camps. So I had no objection to his past politics. But he insisted on being much too dependent on the U.S. And he was slavishly devoted to Secretary of State John Foster Dulles. *He snorts and grimaces.* Those damned Dulles brothers! It was Allen Dulles who insisted on those accursed U-2 flights!

Devil's Advocate: Don't worry. There's a special room in Hell for the Dulles boys – next door to Senator Joe McCarthy and the worst of the House UnAmerican Activities Committee. My boss rarely visits there. S/He figures they are their own worst punishment.

De Gaulle: Justice is best served with irony. *He almost smiles.*

Devil's Advocate: Tell us about the Common Market.

De Gaulle: France and West Germany combined with Italy and the Benelux Countries – Belgium, Netherland, Luxembourg – to form the European Economic Community. Which turned out to be so successful that even the British eventually wanted to join.

Devil's Advocate: And what did you say about that?

De Gaulle: Non.

Devil's Advocate: Um – just 'Non'?

De Gaulle: Oui. 'Non.'

Devil's Advocate: Why?

De Gaulle: As I explained to their Prime Minister, the U.K. was too dependent on the U.S. Sooner or later the former would sell out to the latter.

Devil's Advocate: His reaction?

De Gaulle: He raised the spectre of a newly powerful Germany. I agreed that it was a risk. But we were both continental powers, and had much more resemblance than difference. As continentals, we had before us one and the same menace. For Europeans to cooperate made sense. *Nods approvingly.* England, on the other hand, was insular and maritime, linked through her markets and supply lines to the most diverse and often most distant countries.

Devil's Advocate: So 'Non'.

De Gaulle: Oui. 'Non.' At the time the EEC needed to deepen and accelerate Common Market integration. Not to expand.

Devil's Advocate: 'Europe, from the Atlantic to the Urals'. A favorite rallying cry, n'est-ce pas?

De Gaulle: Yes! My vision was not just for France, but for Europe to become a third pole between USA and USSR. By including territory up to the Urals, I was implicitly offering détente to the Russians. This, of course, was in contrast to the Atlanticism of the Americans and British.

Guardian Angel *takes over the interrogation.* And when did the French people finally stop following you?

De Gaulle: For 11 years I proposed reforms, duly submitted to the people for referendum. I vowed that if they ever voted no, I would resign. Which I did.

Guardian Angel: And then what?

De Gaulle: *(shrugs)* I went home to my modest country home to finish my Memoirs. I was entitled to rather sizeable pensions as a retired President and retired General, but I accepted only a much smaller colonel's pension. My lifestyle required no more. A year after resigning, just before my 80<sup>th</sup> birthday, I died. My health had always been robust, and my death was immediate, without fuss or bother. This was as it should be.

Guardian Angel: You have often been compared to Napoleon. Is that as it should be?

De Gaulle: It's true that both of us rose from modest origins to become 'men of destiny' protecting the glory of France. And both of us were 'men-on-horseback', who provided stable government for the usually contentious French. But Napoleon wanted a French Empire, with Europe under French occupation. I wanted to rescue France and establish a free Europe.

*As* De Gaulle *rises and salutes* Justice, *a huge French tri-color flag unfurls behind. 'La Marseillaise' accompanies him back to the jury box. All rise in respect. Except* LBJ.

# CHAPTER 7

# LYNDON BAINES JOHNSON
# (1908 – 1973)

*Near the jury box, everyone is grouped around* <u>LBJ</u>, *who is telling jokes and mimicking various other politicians they know. He does* Everett Dirksen *extremely well. All are laughing; even* <u>De Gaulle</u> *is smiling.*

<u>Justice</u> *reluctantly returns to Bench. The* <u>Angels</u> *likewise return to their places.*

<u>Justice:</u> Order! (*Residual sounds of mirth, reluctantly suppressed.*) The Court calls Lyndon Baines Johnson, President of the United States.

<u>LBJ</u> *works his way to witness stand, detouring into and pressing the flesh of audience en route.*

<u>Justice:</u> Mr. President, you must not leave Purgatory!

<u>LBJ:</u> Sorry Ma'am, but if there's hands in sight, I can't resist shaking them.

<u>Recording Angel</u> *flashes scene showing baby Lyndon reaching out to everyone, almost leaping out of his Mama's arms. Then fast-forwards through scenes of him working crowds at various stages of his life, always with great gusto. As the years go by, he gets taller and thinner, lanky and dapper, then larger and more commanding to a larger-than-life figure of powerful presence.*

<u>Devil's Advocate</u> *straightens her horns, arranges her cape, then strides to witness stand and smiles engagingly.*
Mr. President, you have quite a reputation. *Smiles again.* I hear you are quite the Wheeler-Dealer.

<u>LBJ</u>: Ma'am, have you ever been to Texas? *He returns her smile, oozing with Southern charm.* That's how things get done.

<u>Devil's Advocate</u>: *(getting down to business)* So to get power, the end justifies the means?

<u>LBJ</u>: If you use the power to make things better for folks, yes.

<u>Devil's Advocate</u>: *(wryly)* And I suppose your ego had nothing to do with it?

<u>LBJ</u>: Nothing wrong with being ambitious. How else could a poor Southern boy end up President of the United States of America!?!

<u>Devil's Advocate</u>: So just how poor was poor?

<u>LBJ</u>: Oh, certainly never dirt poor. And we were always folks of influence. Why, my family was in the state legislature when those Kennedys were still Shanty Irish. *He frowns.* But I had to work my way through State Teacher's College. Never did get one of those fancy Ivy League degrees.

Devil's Advocate: Big guy like you – probably a jock, right?

LBJ: No! (*Scoffs*) Politics was always my thing. *(Shakes his head)* Never could figure out why anyone would waste time playing games that don't matter. Now, politics – that was way more than just a game. What happened <u>did</u> matter. But those guys in sports really thought they were something. Always dated the prettiest girls on campus, too. <u>And</u> they controlled the student activities budget, and made sure athletics got all the cash.

Devil's Advocate: And you fixed that?

LBJ *grins with satisfaction*. I organized all the non-popular people – there were always more of us than them – and we elected a student government that gave all the money to the band and the theatre people – and to my debate team!

Devil's Advocate: And nothing for the athletes?

LBJ: At first, no. But, when they'd learned their lesson, we shared everything equally.

Devil's Advocate: I don't suppose there were any colored folks at your college?

LBJ: No. (*Frowns*) Not back then. Not anywhere in the South.

Devil's Advocate: So back then, you were a racist?

LBJ: Hmmm. (*Frowns again*) I suppose I was. (*Pauses*) But I eventually realized that other things were more important.

Devil's Advocate: How so?

**LBJ:** After I graduated, my first job was teaching at a school full of dirt-poor Mexican kids. They'd never had a chance to be anything. And that just wasn't right! So I started a debate team, and got them all excited. Worked their little brown _____ off. And we ended up state champions. They were proud! And walked tall! *He beams, remembering.* And that's when I decided that every kid should have a chance to be something – didn't matter what color.

**Devil's Advocate:** Was that when you become a supporter of FDR's New Deal?

**LBJ** *nods enthusiastically.* Back in the Depression, things were really hard for almost everyone. But President Roosevelt actually did something about it. And that's why we all started calling him FDR. Respectfully, of course. At first it was so people didn't mix him up with his cousin Teddy Roosevelt. Later it was an expression of affection for a beloved leader – and friend.

**D.A.:** Is that why you started calling yourself LBJ?

**LBJ:** Eventually, yes. He was my hero – because he was right. *He hesitates.* When I got involved in his programs, I realized that if things were to get better for my folks, they had to be better for all folks. And if the South was ever to rejoin the Union – and get out of its economic backwater – we'd have to get beyond the race issue. For too long, too many politicians had been shooting down necessary reform, dividing Southerners by playing the race card. To change that, we finally had to realize that Folks are Folks, no matter what color!

**Guardian Angel:** *smiles encouragingly and takes over questioning.* I'm told you were the best Senate Majority Leader ever.

**LBJ:** Yes, Ma'am! *(nods vigorously.)* That was my favorite job!

<u>Guardian Angel:</u> The Senate got things done because you were able to achieve consensus among all the various factions.

<u>Recording Angel</u> *shows* <u>LBJ</u>, *the cyclone of the Senate, charging down the corridor with aides and reporters tugging at his coat tails, dictating to a secretary trotting to keep up, shaking hands with steelworkers and students en route to his office. His pockets bulging with clippings and memos, he stands at his desk arguing, explaining, compromising, chain-smoking and chain-telephoning. Even sitting, he appears to be moving, flying through a mountain of correspondence, feverishly scratching signatures and postscripts. Working 18-hour days, he gives speeches, goes to meetings, holds press conferences, scans newspapers and yesterday's Congressional Record. He is a tidal wave of activity bursting off the screen and taking over the room.*

<u>Guardian Angel:</u> *(a bit out of breath from chasing her halo)* Whew! Was it always like that?

<u>LBJ</u>: *(grins)* I couldn't have added <u>anything</u> to my schedule without also putting through a bill for a 28-hour day.

*After cleaning up the deluge from her screen,* <u>R.A.Clio</u> *shows a political cartoon of* <u>LBJ</u> *cornering a hapless Senator in a back alley, seizing him by the collar, twisting his arm, dangling a carrot in front of his nose, holding a club over his head.*

<u>LBJ</u> *grins and shrugs.* When you're dealing with all those Senators – the good ones and the crazies, the hard workers and the lazies, the smart ones and the mediocre – you've got to know <u>everything</u> about them – strengths and weakness and aspirations, how far he can be pushed in what direction and by what means. Even how he likes his liquor. I probably knew them better than they knew themselves.

Devil's Advocate *continues the interrogation.* And you used this information to manipulate them? Some say you played the Senate like a skilled harpist.

LBJ: Well, I usually knew which strings to pull – and when.

Devil's Advocate: And if that didn't work?

Recording Angel *shows the 'Johnson Treatment' in action. In the Texas manner,* LBJ *is all over everybody – gripping and tugging and nudging, moving in close, his face literally in the face of his target. Supplication, accusation, cajolery, exuberance, scorn, tears – running the gamut of human emotion at breathtaking velocity, backing his victim into a corner. It is like standing under Niagara Falls in a thunderstorm, leaving the person stunned, as if a great St. Bernard had licked his face for an hour.*

LBJ: Ah, yes, those were the days! Say, maybe I could work out a deal between your boss and (*motions at* G.A.) her boss.

Guardian Angel *chuckles, back at her desk.* I'll mention it to my supervisor. But I'm not sure even S/He could withstand the Johnson Treatment.

Devil's Advocate *laughs too, then gets serious.* But did you use this potent weapon responsibly?

LBJ: I tried to. Especially in ridding the South of the curse of racism! Early on I looked at how blacks and Hispanics lived, and saw that they didn't have a decent chance for good health and housing and jobs. They were always skating right on the edge, struggling to keep body and soul together. And I often thought that someday I would love to help those people – to give them a chance.

Devil's Advocate: And as a powerful Senator, you were finally in a position to do it.

LBJ: No one but me could have gotten that first Civil Rights bill through Congress. Jim Crow put a collar on lots of smart men as sure as if they were sentenced to a chain gang in Georgia. Some of the other Southern Senators could have been President instead of me. How could they throw that away for the sake of hating?! *He furrows his brow and shakes his head.*

Devil's Advocate*:* So why did you give up a job with real power for the least powerful job in D.C.?

LBJ: Because I wanted to eventually be President. *Pauses, then shrugs.* And because John Kennedy asked for my help. He needed me to deliver Texas.

Devil's Advocate: Was being Vice-President as bad as they say?

LBJ: Worse. *(Sighs)* Though I did get a chance to see the world.

Recording Angel's *screen shows Lyndon walking in a fishing village in Senegal, handing out pens and lighters, shaking hands with everyone – including a few fingerless lepers, advising bewildered natives that they could be like Texans and increase their annual income tenfold in 40 years.*

*Then Lyndon repeatedly stopping a motorcade into Saigon, shaking hands with South Vietnamese, giving children passes to the U.S. Senate gallery, exhorting them to 'get your mamma and daddy to bring you to the Congress and see how government works.'*

*Next, Lyndon strolling the streets of Bangkok, patting children on the head, entering a store and lecturing non-English speaking customers on the virtues of democracy and dangers of Chinese Communists.*

*Lyndon testing the acoustics of the Taj Mahal with a Texas cowboy whoop.*

*Lyndon discovering a herd of Texas cattle in a Seoul suburb, chasing them around the pasture to get a good photo-op with the steers.*

*And so on. And on.*

Devil's Advocate: You invited lots of these people to visit. Did any of them take you up on it?

LBJ *chuckles.* There was one in Pakistan I especially remember. On the way into Karachi, I was shaking hands as usual, and spotted a barefoot man with a camel. He had a fine face, so I leaped across a muddy ditch to shake his hand and said 'Y'all come visit in the United States. The next day, Bashir Ahmad the camel driver was in the headlines of the local newspapers. Back home, I got a call from the American Embassy in Pakistan that the now famous camel driver's visit had better happen or we would lose face.

*Lyndon gets into telling the story in typical Texas style, with lots of gestures and mimicking. As usual, his acting fills the room.*

Well, the government was afraid that an illiterate peasant would embarrass them, so they arrested the poor guy and had him hidden somewhere. Then the s__t really hit the fan. There was a huge public outcry. So I directly appealed to the President of Pakistan to free Bashir.

*Over in the jury box* Nehru *is smiling hugely.*

Devil's Advocate: And how was the visit?

LBJ: We found a good translator, who turned everything Bashir said into beautiful little homilies. He was a hit, and got a pickup truck donated by Ford Motors.

*Everyone is laughing.*

*LBJ, energized by his performance, pulls pens inscribed with his name from his pockets, and passes them out to everyone. To* Churchill, *he also slips one of his labeled lighters Then he returns to witness stand.*

All those foreign places I visited – lots of good folks to shake hands with. *He brightens.* Folks are folks anywhere, but I was always more comfortable back home.

Devil's Advocate: *(with a sly smile)* And how did you get along with the Kennedy crowd?

LBJ: *(Obviously this is a sore spot.)* Pretty much they ignored me. Or looked down their snooty Ivy League noses at me. *Frowns, considering.* I never did figure it out. Here was a whippersnapper, never said or did much of importance in the Senate. But somehow there was this image of a shining young leader who would change the face of the country. Yes, he had a good sense of humor and looked awfully good on the damn television screen… I just looked awful – no matter what I did. *Shakes his head.* But his hold on the American public is still a mystery to me. *Frowns again.* That boy Jack didn't have enough experience to be President. Though he did better than I expected and certainly meant well. He always treated me with respect. But that Bobby…! *With difficulty he suppresses a long colorful string of words unacceptable in Purgatory.* But they had the right ideas – which all got stuck in the Senate. They should have asked me to help. I could have gotten them through. And did when I became President.

<u>Devil's Advocate:</u> And the assassination? Was that your doing?

<u>LBJ:</u> H____, no! I know a lot of people thought so, but I was as shocked as anyone. And felt real bad for Mrs. Kennedy and the children. Lady Bird and I tried to help however we could. And we gave her as much time as she needed to move out of the White House.

<u>Devil's Advocate:</u> But when you moved in, surely that must have been satisfying.

<u>LBJ</u> *opens his mouth to protest, remembers where he is, then remains silent.*

<u>Devil's Advocate</u> *returns to her desk;* <u>Guardian Angel</u> *approaches witness stand.*

<u>G. A.:</u> That must have been a difficult time for your country.

<u>LBJ:</u> *(nodding vehemently in agreement)* The entire nation was grieving for this bright young man, who had filled them with so much hope. But the country – and the world – needed to know that someone was still in charge. Meanwhile, tribute had to be paid to the fallen leader.

<u>Guardian Angel:</u> And how did you manage this?

<u>LBJ:</u> I finished President Kennedy's term in memoriam. I kept the members of his Cabinet, and pushed <u>all</u> those bills of his, stalled in committee, through Congress.

<u>Guardian Angel:</u> That must have pleased his family and friends.

LBJ: *(frowning)* Yeah, you'd think so. I gave them everything he promised – and more. But somehow they never gave me credit for it. 'Oh, that's just Lyndon playing politics again.' They never understood that I was politicking because I wanted to do right for folks. *Shakes his head, still wondering.*

Guardian Angel: And then you ran for President on your own.

Recording Angel *shows scenes of* LBJ *campaigning, motorcades passing through huge friendly crowds thick as molasses, cheering everything he says, supporting his moderation and affinity for the political center. Even in the South he courageously confronts the race issue head on: 'Prosperity must know no Mason-Dixon line and opportunity no color line.' He is like Joshua summoning the trumpets at Jericho.*

LBJ: *(grinning broadly)* I won by the biggest landslide vote ever. I took it as a mandate for my Great Society program. My whole career was built on the belief that federal money well spent on infrastructure, social programs, and defense, could serve the national well-being – especially in the underdeveloped South. And now I had the chance to carry on FDR's legacy.

Guardian Angel: And once you got going there was no stopping you. Congress passed more bills than during any other session in its history.

Recording Angel *recites list of Great Society Bills passed as screen shows* LBJ *working Congress, getting it to move.*
>
> Aid to Education
> Medicare
> Voting Rights
> Housing Act

*As President he is constantly telephoning and conferring and pressuring reluctant Representatives and Senator.*
> Fair Immigration Law
> Mental Health Facilities
> Vocational Rehabilitation
> Anti-Poverty Program

*The Johnson Treatment is in full flower, ratchetted up several notches by the power vested in the Oval Office.*
> Arts and Humanities Foundation
> Water Pollution Control
> Clean Air
> High Speed Transit

*His finger pounding the chest of uncooperative Congressman,* LBJ *gives him a 3-minute lesson in Integrity – and then promises to ruin him.*
> Aid to Small Business
> Teachers Corps
> Freedom of Information
> Law Enforcement Assistance

*In D.C., E=mc2 is replaced by E=LBJ. It is said that if AirForce One runs out of fuel, his energy would keeping it flying.*
> New GI Bill
> Public Broadcasting
> Truth-in-Lending
> Colorado River Reclamation

*And on and on, until finally* R.A.Clio *stops, exhausted.*

LBJ: *(Proudly)* And there were lots more.

*All the occupants in the jury box are marveling at all these impressive legislative achievements.*

*Especially* <u>De Gaulle:</u> Monsieur le President, I salute your skill at subduing the passions of those who breed disorderly dissension. I wonder how you would deal with the French Parlement. Mon Dieu, but that would be something to see!

<u>Guardian Angel:</u> Of all these laws, which was the most difficult to pass?

<u>LBJ:</u> The second Civil Rights Bill. The first one was just a foot in the door, but this one had real teeth. And then, of course, the Voting Rights Act. The South fought it all the way – and never did forgive me. But it was so long overdue. It <u>had</u> to happen. And I was going to be the President who finished what Lincoln began!

*He stands, remembering. As the Court of Purgatory transforms into the House Chamber of the U.S. Capitol, he recites his memorable speech to Congress.*

Rarely in any time does an issue lay bare the secret heart of America itself. Rarely are we met with a challenge to the values and the purposes and the meaning of our beloved Nation. The issue of equal rights is such an issue. And should we defeat every enemy, should we double our wealth and conquer the stars, and still be unequal to this issue, then we will have failed as a people and as a nation.

*As he stops reading his script, his leaden 'presidential' delivery falls away and reveals the passion of the real Lyndon.*

The issue is democracy, the right of the individual, regardless of race or color, to vote. The command of the Constitution is plain. It is wrong – deadly wrong – to deny any of your fellow Americans the right to vote in this country. There is no issue of states rights or national rights. There is only the struggle for human rights. Because really it is all of us, who must overcome the crippling legacy of bigotry and injustice. And, *he pauses, raising his arms for emphasis,* WE SHALL OVERCOME!

*A moment of stunned silence follows. Then almost the entire chamber rises in unison, applauding, shouting, stamping their feet. Senators, congressmen, observers in the gallery are moved by joy that the victor, for a change, is human decency.*

*The standing ovation goes on and on.*

*Everyone in Court stands and joins in, cheering and applauding.*

*Fade out light and ovation.*

*Darkness and silence for a few minutes, then Fade In.*

<u>LBJ</u> *is again seated in Witness Chair, being interrogated by* <u>Devil's Advocate</u>, *who is still wiping away her tears.*

<u>Devil's Advocate:</u> It looks like you were a cinch to be a Hero of History. And for admission to Heaven. So what happened to get my boss so interested?

<u>LBJ:</u> VIET-NAM!!!

<u>Recording Angel</u> *shows scenes of bombs raining from U.S. planes destroying villages, greasy billowing fireballs of napalm defoliating the countryside, Buddhist monks self-immolating in protest. Finally, after more explosives than all those used in World War II have been expended to 'save' the Vietnamese from Communism, the country is totally devastated.*

<u>Devil's Advocate:</u> *(sardonically)* You had the most powerful armies and weapons in all human history, and here you were

picking on this little country in Southeast Asia. I guess you didn't care about folks who were yellow.

LBJ: Oh yes! We did! We were trying to save them from Communism! First Stalin grabbed Eastern Europe. Then the Reds took over China. And just like North Korea invaded South Korea, Communist North Vietnam was threatening South Vietnam. If they won, the rest of Southeast Asia would fall like a row of dominoes. We couldn't give in to the Commies like when Hitler was allowed to take Czechoslovakia. That kind of Appeasement caused World War II.

Khrushchev: (*leaping up and snorting with exasperation*) Why must you Americans be so ignorant of what happened? You did far worse to Vietnam than anything we did to Eastern Europe! Why can't you ever look at things through someone else's eyes?! Why don't you just look at a map once in awhile?! *He throws up his hands in disgust.* Your history books are even worse than ours!

Justice: Order in the Court!

Khrushchev *sits down, muttering angrily, and gradually subsides.*

LBJ: But the Domino Theory, Munich and Appeasement, this is what everyone believed back then.

Devil's Advocate: But after years and years of bombing and burning, fighting and killing, Ho Chi Minh finally won.

LBJ *shakes his head.* I still can't figure out how that happened.

De Gaulle *rises majestically.* I warned President Kennedy that this would happen, that intervention in this area would be an endless entanglement. Once a nation has been aroused, no foreign power, however strong, can impose its will. The ideology you invoke will make no difference. In the eyes of the masses it will be identified with your will to power. That is why the more you become involved out there against Communism, the more the Communists will appear as the champions of national independence.

LBJ: Did Kennedy believe you?

De Gaulle: He listened. *Shrugs.* We French learned from disastrous experience. You Americans foolishly took our place in Vietnam. You wanted to take over where we left off and revive a war which we brought to an end by leaving. I predicted that you would sink step by step into a bottomless military and political quagmire, however much you spent in men and money.

LBJ: But we couldn't just let them go Communist!

De Gaulle: What we all should do for Asia is not to take over the running of these States ourselves, but to provide them with the means to escape from the misery which is the cause of totalitarian regimes.

LBJ *uncharacteristically almost intimidated, finally comments.* If it had been up to me, we wouldn't have gotten involved. Foreign Policy was never my thing. Foreigners are not like the folks I am used to. But we were there, and I thought we had to keep our word. And most Americans thought it was the right thing to do.

Devil's Advocate: When you became President, there were only American "advisors" in Vietnam. No bombing then, or ground troops actually fighting. Why escalate?

LBJ: All those Harvard advisors I inherited from Kennedy said so. They sounded so sure, and they knew more about the world than I did. And who could resist that brilliant Robert McNamara!

*On* <u>Recording Angel</u>*'s screen is* Robert McNamara, *Secretary of Defense, his stay-comb hair parted off-center and slicked back. Whether meetings of Pentagon Generals or Presidential advisors, he is surrounded by charts and graphs, to which he points while rattling off numbers and figures at lightening speed. He tolerates no dissent, and barks at those who have the temerity to disagree.*

<u>Devil's Advocate:</u> So it was McNamara's fault?

<u>LBJ:</u> H\_\_\_, no! I was President! Like Harry Truman said, 'The Buck Stops Here.'

<u>R.A.Clio</u> *whispers angrily in D.A.'s ear.*

<u>Devil's Advocate:</u> Clio says McNamara had absolutely NO sense of history. And that any college kid with a computer could do his number-crunching. So how did you get taken in by this one-dimensional statistician?

<u>LBJ:</u> Because everyone thought he was one of the best and brightest – Government, Corporations, Wall Street – that's even what Harvard was teaching its MBAs!

<u>Devil's Advocate:</u> But eventually even McNamara doubted the wisdom of all the escalation of men and weapons ordered into Vietnam, and quit as Secretary of Defense. Why didn't you get out then?

<u>LBJ:</u> (*after a very long pause*) Because by that time it was <u>My</u> war! <u>My</u> planes! <u>My boys!</u>

*Pauses again.* And I wasn't going to be the only President to ever lose a war!

*The D.A. hands the interrogation over to the G.A.*

Guardian Angel: You could have run again in 1968. Why didn't you?

LBJ: It wasn't so much the Protesters – all that didn't get really going until later into Nixon's term. But no matter what we did in Vietnam, it didn't work. And they were my boys dying!

Guardian Angel: You announced several months before the election that you wouldn't seek re-election. Was there a purpose in that?

LBJ: I thought if I just concentrated on negotiating a settlement with the North Vietnamese we could somehow get out with honor. If I kept politics completely out of it, maybe I could at least get them to the table to talk.

Guardian Angel: Did it work?

LBJ: We came close. I finally dealt with the Vietnamese – North and South – like I did Congress. And pretty much locked in a deal to start negotiations. But the Nixon Campaign sabotaged the effort. Somehow he sent a message that if they waited until he got elected, they would get a better deal from him.

Guardian Angel: And did they?

LBJ: H____, no! He escalated it more and more. Meanwhile our country was torn apart, pro and con. And then finally he pulled out anyway.

<u>Recording Angel</u> *shows university campuses all over the country exploding into protest, 'Hell no! We won't go!', National Guard firing on students burning draft cards, young men fleeing to Canada, arguing with fathers who are World War II veterans.*

*Finally the screen shows U.S. helicopters taking off from roof of American Embassy, leaving behind thousands of panicking South Vietnamese dependents, as North Vietnamese army, many on bicycles, moves into Saigon.*

<u>LBJ</u> *sits silent with bowed head, then speaks with difficulty.* Some men want power simply to strut around the world and hear 'Hail to the Chief'. Well, I wanted power to give things to people – all sorts of things to all sorts of people who needed help. Everyone thought I was a power-hungry monster. But all I really wanted was to make things better for folks... Where did I go wrong?......

*Fade out.*

# CHAPTER 8

# ENDGAME

*All players are in jury box. Whereas in previous appearances each has been in his prime, now they are all old men. Physically and mentally, however, they are in various stages of deterioration.*

Justice: Oyez, oyez, oyez! The Court of Purgatory is now in session. (*Pauses and smiles*) I always wanted to say that! (*Looks over at jury box*)

One of the perks of being in Purgatory is that you get to see your own funeral. (*Murmuring and quiet exclamations from jury box.*)

But first we will see the end of your lives – and relive your dying.

(*Groans from Churchill, Khrushchev and LBJ.*)

**Scene 1: Churchill** (1965 – Age 91)

Justice: Sir Winston, since you are the oldest of our elder statesmen, we will start with you.

Churchill *growls as his wheelchair is pushed next to the Witness Stand. The usual cigar is drooping from his mouth as he slowly fumbles in his pockets for something with which to light it.*

Justice: (*in a voice louder than usual*) Sir Winston, this is a no-smoking zone, remember?

Churchill: What was that? *Looks blank for a moment, then stops rummaging in his pockets.* Oh yes – bloody stupid rule. *His speech is slow and slightly slurred.*

Devil's Advocate: Don't worry, Sir Winston. If my boss has her way, you soon won't have to worry about finding a light.

Churchill: *His combative gleam abruptly returns.* And does he have any good whiskey down there?!

Devil's Advocate: (*smiles*) Yes, I believe S/He does.

Churchill *harrumphs in usual British fashion.*

Devil's Advocate: Clio tells me that you had the biggest state funeral in history.

Churchill *grins as in World War II days and makes an unsteady V for Victory.*
That's as it should be!

*He searches unsuccessfully for a witty remark.*

*Finally the 'black dog' of Depression reasserts itself.*
But they certainly made me wait for it! For the past 12 years I've been like this! I even had to resign from my 2$^{nd}$ term as Prime Minister. Had to leave the job to – who was that young man? *He struggles to remember.*

132

<u>Devil's Advocate:</u> *(After a polite pause)* Anthony Eden.

<u>Churchill:</u> *(Brightens)* Yes, Anthony Eden! That's the one – Anthony Eden.

<u>Devil's Advocate</u>: Are you ready to see your funeral? They seem to have trotted out all the pomp and circumstance of the British Empire.

<u>Churchill</u>: And why not? Who else worked harder to maintain the glory of the Empire?

<u>Devil's Advocate</u>: Even after it was time to let go?

<u>Churchill</u> *glowers at her, then eagerly turns his attention to the* <u>Recording Angel's</u> *screen.*

<u>R.A.Clio</u> *shows Churchill's body lying in state in Westminster Abbey, then transported, amid Royal troops of red-coated be-plumed trotting Horse Guards, to St. Paul's Cathedral for the Funeral, attended by emissaries from 112 nations, excepting only China and Ireland. Even the Queen is there. Afterward, the coffin passes up the Thames river, while the Royal Artillery fires a 19-gun salute, and the RAF stages a fly-over of 16 Fighter Planes. At Waterloo Station the coffin is loaded aboard a specially painted railway carriage. As the train passes slowly to the final burial place, thousands stand silently paying their respects. He is finally interred in the family plot at St. Martin's Church, not far from his birthplace in Blenheim Palace, ancestral home of his grandfather, the Duke of Marlborough.*

<u>Churchill</u>: *(Quietly weeping)* Ah, those were the days.

<u>Devil's Advocate</u>: How many of your colleagues here were at your funeral?

Khrushchev: Not me, I was in exile.

Nehru: Not me, I was already dead.

LBJ: I sent Hubert Humphrey. He was Vice-President, so it was his turn to do that sort of thing.

De Gaulle: Of course I was there!

*He stands. The scene fades into Westminster Abbey, its thick stone walls muffling the howling gale outside. He walks slowly up the aisle, his footsteps echoing in the empty church. His long greatcoat and the crown of his kepi are wind whipped with cold rain. He stands at attention, facing the flag-draped catafalque.*

*Finally he speaks:* You and I were thrust into leadership by the failure of others. And together we saved our nations from the darkness of the Nazis. There is no one with whom I would rather have fought this noble fight. Oh, you were often a difficult ally – currying favor with Roosevelt at my expense, dividing up Europe with Stalin behind everyone's back, stealing Syria from us under cover of war... Yes, I knew what you were up to, you old fox... But I could never have saved France without your help.

So farewell, my comrade-in-arms. I, too, am becoming an anachronism. And shall soon join you. But I leave behind my beloved France, stronger for having shed the burden of Empire. As for England, can you say the same?

*He salutes, about-faces, walks back up the aisle as Westminster Abbey fades back into the Court of Purgatory.*

*As* De Gaulle *sits down,* Churchill *squirms in his wheelchair and shouts angrily:*

There will always be England!

*He struggles to hear 'God Save the Queen', but there is only silence.*

*In disbelief, he repeats:* There will always be England!... Won't there?

*Fade out.*

**Scene 2: Nehru** (1964, Age 75)

Justice: The Court calls Jawaharlal Nehru, Prime Minister of India.

Nehru *walks rather slowly to witness stand, wearing his usual Nehru jacket and Gandhi cap. Slightly heavier, he is nonetheless still in good shape for a man of 75. But extreme fatigue permeates his body; his shoulders droop and his eyes are filled with sadness. Even so, he greets the Court with his usual 'Namaste'.*

Guardian Angel: Mr. Nehru, unlike your colleagues here, you died while still in office.

Nehru: *(smiles ruefully)* Not entirely by choice. I tried to resign several times, but they wouldn't let me. And even though I refused special security, the numerous assassination attempts were not successful, either.

Guardian Angel: Seems like it was your destiny to lead India all your life.

Nehru: *(sighs)* Had I found an effective replacement I would have resigned. *(Shakes his head.)* There were plenty of able men out there. The problem was that they had the allegiance of only part of the nation. There were so many groups of different languages

135

and religions and traditions and ethnic groups. Throughout my 17 years as Prime Minister I constantly exhorted local leaders to 'Integrate or Perish'. But none of them seemed able to represent all of India.

Guardian Angel: So you stayed in office?

Nehru: Longer than I should have. And left no designated successor. I regret that.

Guardian Angel: You look very tired.

Nehru: Mentally and physically, my robust constitution served me well. But my heart was broken by Zhou Enlai's betrayal. And my poor judgment left my people unprotected against the Chinese attack. As their leader, I failed them. *Bows his head.*

Guardian Angel: That time, yes. But Clio tells me that more often than not, you served them well. And that you always had their love and respect.

Nehru: (*Smiles*) Which they showed me so often I felt no need for an elaborate funeral. So I requested that my ashes be sent to Allahabad, where a handful should be thrown into the Ganges, the river of India, ever-changing, ever-flowing and ever the same.

Guardian Angel: What about the rest of your ashes?

Nehru: (*slightly embarrassed*) Well, perhaps I was a bit romantic about that. I wanted them to be carried high up in an aeroplane and scattered over the fields where the peasants toil, so that they might mingle with the dust and soil and become part of India.

Guardian Angel: Well, let's see if they respected your wishes.

<u>Recording Angel</u>'s *screen shows the Indian Parliament. 'The Prime Minister is dead,' announces the Speaker. 'The Light is no more.' The members weep openly. Newspaper headlines all mourn: 'The Light has gone out of our lives, and there is darkness everywhere.'*

*The scene shifts to Nehru's residence in New Delhi. Inside, his body lies in state on a sloping catafalque, draped in the saffron, white and green flag of India. During the night, a million villagers in turbans and women carrying babies wait in line with officials, princes, diplomats to move slowly by the body. Outside, a huge crowd surges and stampedes the main gate; 3 people die and 12 are injured in the crush.*

*Shortly before the funeral procession starts, there is an earthquake. Undeterred, the cortege moves 6 miles up Rajpath, past the Parliament building, then on to the rajghat on the river Jumna. Weeping millions line the route in the stifling heat, crowds so dense the procession can hardly move. Scores are injured. Surrounded by a great mound of flowers and sobs of anguished mourners, Nehru lies on a gun carriage drawn by sixty men of the armed forces.*

*At the rajghat, the body is placed on a pyre; family and friends and old comrades pile sticks of sandalwood underneath. Countless wreaths are brought by visiting statesmen, making a garden of flowers around the body. Lord Mountbatten, India's last Viceroy, and the British Prime Minister are there, as is Alexei Kosygin from Russia and Dean Rusk, U.S. Secretary of State.*

*Nehru's grandson lights the pyre; flames leap into the air, laden with the scent of jasmine. The fire blazes higher, as crowds press forward throwing rose petals and sacred water into the flames.*

*The ashes finally cool and are placed in an urn, carried by the Family aboard a special train to Allahabad. All along hundreds of miles of track, millions of weeping mourners pay tribute. At*

*Allahabad, some of the ashes are scattered in the Ganges. The rest are sown from a small airplane flying East to West, North to South.*

*The screen fades.*

<u>Nehru</u> *is weeping quietly.*

<u>Guardian Angel</u>: (*wiping her eyes*) It appears that your instructions were followed.

<u>Nehru</u>: (*smiling*) Yes, and I'm relieved that none of my ashes were preserved. I did not want them to build a monument for people to worship.

<u>Guardian Angel</u>: Well – um – about that...

*She reluctantly signals* <u>Recording Angel</u> *to show picture of a peaceful, rather modest garden. In the center is a broad circular mound of green grass, surrounded by a wide walkway. Small groups of quiet people walk there, pausing to pay sincere respects. Some take off their shoes.*

<u>Nehru</u>: What's this?!

<u>Guardian Angel</u>: (*quietly*) It's your memorial.

<u>Nehru</u>: (*sighs*) But I specifically said –

<u>Guardian Angel</u>: (*interrupts*) Yes, but people insisted. Your daughter at least tried to keep it understated.

<u>Nehru</u>: Yes, that's true.

<u>Guardian Angel</u>: But no one could stop people all over India from erecting statues of you and naming streets after you. Lots

of stadiums, too. And just about every other school is named for you.

Khrushchev: (*grinning*) I think there's even a Russian postage stamp with your picture on it.

Nehru *smiles, and the sadness leaves his eyes. He departs the witness stand with a lighter step.*

**Scene 3: De Gaulle** (1970, Age 80)

Justice: The Court calls General Charles De Gaulle, President of the French Republic.

De Gaulle *marches to witness stand, salutes the Court, then unbends into the chair. His girth is noticeably wider than in the days of the Resistance, but his erect carriage and even step are indicative of still robust health.*

Justice: Monsieur le General, you were President – for the second time – for 11 years, n'est-ce pas?

De Gaulle: Oui, Mme de Justice.

Justice: And you voluntarily relinquished power about a year before your death?

De Gaulle: C'est vrai, Madame. I had always told the French that I would serve as long as they gave me the power to do what needed to be done. I periodically called for a referendum so the people could indicate support for my policies. When the vote finally went against me, I promptly resigned. Just as I had always promised.

Justice: And then?

De Gaulle: I retired to my modest country estate in Colombey-les-Deux-Eglises, about 120 miles SE of Paris, lived on a colonel's pension, and wrote my Memoirs.

Justice: Surely you were entitled to something more?

De Gaulle: (*shrugs*) Mais oui. But I didn't need it. As always, I lived simply. And died without a fuss – a sudden stroke, I recall, while watching the news and playing solitaire. And requested a simple funeral to match. Mass in the local church, attended only by family and Compagnons de la Liberation.

Justice: What about the presidents and ministers, dignitaries and heads of state? Were they invited?

De Gaulle: Non. No politicians. No diplomats. Pas de tout. I served only France.

Justice: Clio tells me that your wish for a private funeral was honored. But so great was the outcry from the French – and the world – that a memorial service was held simultaneously at Notre Dame in Paris. People came from all over to pay their respects. It was, in fact, the biggest such event in French History.

De Gaulle: (*frowns*) They should have been paying their respects to France.

Recording Angel *turns on screen. From the small Catholic church at Colombey, the picture pans out to the surrounding countryside. All of the roads for miles around are clogged with thousands of cars. The fields are filled with hundreds of thousands of French people, many with blankets and picnic baskets.*

*The scene shifts to Paris, where Notre Dame is filled with heads of state –– past and present –– from all over the world. Outside,*

*Parisian crowds are packed so tightly that those who faint have to be passed overhead to first-aid stations in the rear.*

*The service in Notre Dame is coordinated with the Mass at Colombey. At the moment De Gaulle's body is lowered into his grave, the bells of the church begin to toll, followed immediately by the bells of Notre Dame. Soon all the bells of all the churches all over France are tolling. The bells ring out for a long time –- in gratitude to the man who saved France: from Nazis, from colonialism, from superpowers – and from themselves.*

De Gaulle: *Tears rolling slowly in precise formation down his cheeks, he stands.*
Vive la France!

*When everyone is seated,* R.A.Clio's *screen shows a small gravestone in the modest cemetery of the Colombey church. It is plain, surmounted only by a cross, and is inscribed simply 'Charles De Gaulle, 1890-1970'.*

Nehru: (*smiling*) I congratulate the French for obeying your orders, General. I see no worshipful monuments to your memory.

Recording Angel: Well – um – not quite.
*She shows the huge international airport in Paris.* They named this after you and this, too. *She shows a French nuclear-powered aircraft carrier.* There are also statues of you all over – even in places like Warsaw and Moscow and Quebec. And there appear to be streets named for you in virtually every country of the world.

De Gaulle: (*hesitates*) And what of the French?

Recording Angel: In the French pantheon of heroes, you are placed ahead of Napoleon – behind only Charlemagne.

*On the screen is the French Tri-Color.* De Gaulle *stands, all 6'6" of him, at attention, and salutes his flag.*

*Fade out.*

### Scene 4: Khrushchev (1971, Age 77)

Justice: The Court calls Nikita Sergeevich Khrushchev, General Secretary of the Communist Party of the Soviet Union.

Khrushchev *very slowly walks to witness stand, minus the usual bear hugs and noisy kisses. The strenuous circumstances of his life have finally caught up with his heart and body. He is massively depressed, all exuberance gone. The disappearance of his buoyant personality underscores how short he is.*

Recording Angel Clio: Comrade Khrushchev, the circumstances of your retirement are rather different from those of your colleagues. Unlike Sir Winston, General De Gaulle, and President Johnson, you did not retire voluntarily. Nor did you die in office as did Prime Minister Nehru.

Khrushchev: (*shrugs*) But of course. These things are different in Russia. To get power, you usually have to kill whoever already has it.

R.A.Clio: But you changed that, didn't you?

Khrushchev: When Party Officials told me I was through, I didn't fight them. I was old and tired. But could anyone have dreamed of telling Stalin that he didn't suit us anymore and suggesting he retire? Not even a wet spot would have remained where he was standing. *He shrugs again.* That was my contribution.

R.A.Clio: So they allowed you to live.

Khrushchev: Yes, and they didn't even send me to Siberia. I was given a decent pension, a small apartment in Moscow, and a modest dacha in the nearby countryside. There were, of course, KGB guards at the gate – taking careful note of whoever came to visit. So there weren't many visitors. And I needed permission to leave.

R.A.Clio: And was it given?

Khrushchev: Sometimes. But the problem was that I was not allowed to do anything. I spent my whole life protecting my country and building Socialism. I had been around and knew a lot. But they wouldn't let me share any of that. So where was there to go?

R.A.Clio: Were you allowed access to information about the outside world?

Khrushchev: As much as any ordinary citizen. And enough to see that the new people in power were undoing much of what I had tried to do. Many of the Collective Farms even stopped planting corn. And that fool Brezhnev started building as many missiles as the Americans thought we actually had. With me, it had mostly been a bluff to allow shifting from guns to butter. But with the new regime, it was real. And that's when the arms race began to get out of control.

R.A.Clio: Did you try to stop it?

Khrushchev: How could I? I no longer even existed. I was made such a nonperson that my very name was erased from the history books. They even airbrushed out pictures of me greeting cosmonauts and visiting dignitaries. There's Yuri Gagarin – or Van Cliburn – shaking hands with an empty space. Probably some of you there, too. (*Points at jury box*) And lots of empty spots on top of Lenin's Mausoleum reviewing the troops.

R.A.Clio: (*gently*) I can assure you, Comrade Khrushchev, that History will not forget you.

Khrushchev: (*looking up in surprise*) That's what my son kept telling me. And he urged me to write my Memoirs. Which, at first, I was too depressed to even consider. Then one day I overheard someone ask my young grandson 'Nikita, what does your grandfather do all day?' He answered, 'Grandfather cries.' *Tears slowly run down his cheeks.* It was true. So I decided to leave my grandchildren some better memories.

R.A.Clio: Most of your peers wrote their Memoirs, too. Why was it so much harder for you?

Khrushchev: Of course I had no access to a library – and all my papers had been confiscated when I was deposed. So everything had to be what I remembered. Fortunately, my memory is very good. *He grins.* Since I've never been able to write as fast as I think, I've always dictated what I had to say. So my son brought me a tape recorder, and I started talking.

R.A.Clio: I assume that your living quarters were bugged?

Khrushchev: Of course. (*shrugs*) But now, what did it matter? And at least someone was listening to what I knew. Maybe even passing it along to someone who might make good use of it.

R.A.Clio: Did they ever try to stop you?

Khrushchev: No, but I knew they would eventually take the tapes. And the thought of my life just getting buried somewhere...

R.A.Clio: Is that when you decided to smuggle copies of the tapes to the West?

Khrushchev: (*reluctantly*) Yes. (*pauses*) Please understand. I did not intend this to hurt my country. I just knew that it was the only way Russians would ever be able to read about what I tried to do – and to learn from my mistakes.

R.A.Clio: And when the Memoirs were finished?

Khrushchev: All those marathon drunken parties with Stalin caught up with me. I was in and out of hospitals with various ailments. Until my heart finally quit.

R.A.Clio: Here is your obituary. *She flashes up one line on the back page of 'Pravda' that 'expresses sorrow at the death of honorable pensioner Nikita Sergeevich Khrushchev.'*

Khrushchev: That's it?... Well, it's more than I expected.

R.A.Clio: And I'm sure you won't be surprised that you had no state funeral nor that you were not interred in the wall of The Kremlin.

Khrushchev: So where did they put me?

R.A.Clio: In the cemetery of the Novodevichy Convent.

Khrushchev: Humhh. *He is surprised. But not displeased.*

R.A.Clio: You have some interesting neighbors there.

Khrushchev: Yes, I know. But they probably weren't enthused about me joining them.

R.A.Clio: Well, let's see.

*She turns on her screen. En route to Khrushchev's grave are several remarkably creative tombstones, with their occupants perched on top: Chekhov and Mayakovsky, Prokofiev and Shostakovich, Stanislavsky and Eisenstein, Tupelev and Ilyushin, among others. All are smiling and waving in welcome.*

Khrushchev: Amazing. (*Shakes his head, wondering.*) But why?

R.A.Clio: They all know what you did about censorship. Letting 'Ivan Denisovich' be published was courageous.

Khrushchev: But I don't see Solzhenitsyn anywhere.

R.A.Clio: He isn't dead yet.

*The path stops in front of Khrushchev's tombstone. It is a large modern sculpture with abstract forms opposing each other. White marble bears down on black granite, which resists and struggles and refuses to yield. In between is a gold model of Khrushchev's head. In the upper corner is a symbolic sun with rays extending downward, dispelling the darkness.*

Khrushchev: Well... the head is a pretty good likeness... But I'm not sure what the rest of it is supposed to be.

Eisenstein: (*stepping in front of his camera*) It represents the antagonism between light and dark, progressive and dynamic vs. reactionary and static. One strains to move forward, the other pulls back. This is your life, Nikita Sergeevich. You began to lead our country out of darkness. The dawn broke for all of us, as light began to dispel darkness.

Khrushchev *smiles whole-heartedly – at last.* Really?? That's what you see? Yes! Yes! That's what I tried to do. *He looks around.* Did one of you make this?

Eisenstein: No. He's not dead yet, either. His name is Neizvestny.

Khrushchev: Oh, I remember him. *He frowns.* His work was at a Modern Art exhibit some idiot in the Artists' Union persuaded me to attend. It was decadent Western stuff. I hated it! (*Grins, but a bit embarrassed.*) I even called it dog-s__t!

R.A.Clio: Obviously, he forgave you. *She points approvingly at his tombstone.*

Khrushchev: What a fine fellow! *He beams and bounces a bit.* I like this! Definitely not dog-s__t! (*Grins.*) And I like my neighbors here. (*Waves at all of them.*) So what kind of funeral did I get?

R.A.Clio: It was a simple graveside interment, which wasn't announced until the last minute. Fearful of possible demonstrations, the cemetery was surrounded by government troops. Even so, some artists and writers managed to join your family for the burial. Shortly after, the cemetery itself was closed. The authorities were afraid of an unofficial shrine developing around your grave.

Khrushchev: After all I did to denounce Stalin's Cult of Personality, I certainly hope nothing like that happened.

R.A.Clio: (*Smiles*) Here – see for yourself what happens every October 14ᵗʰ on the anniversary of your being deposed.

*The screen shows the Novodevichy Cemetery, closed and guarded. But at midnight, small groups of old men and women start slipping silently through holes in the fence. Each lays a single flower on Khrushchev's grave. These are the people who were freed when he opened the gates of the Gulag. By morning, the gravesite is covered by mounds of fresh flowers.*

Khrushchev *watches, his smile breaking forth from torrents of tears.*

Clio *and* Justice *are also smiling.*

*Scene fades.*

## Scene 5 – LBJ (1973, Age 65)

Justice: The Court calls Lyndon B. Johnson, President of the United States.

LBJ *walks slowly to witness stand, not shaking any hands en route. He is overweight and pulling an oxygen tank. He pats his left pocket to make sure the nitroglycerin tablets are handy; in his right pocket is a pack of cigarettes. His usual neatly barbered hair is swept back in shoulder length silver curls. Except for the long hair, he looks much older than his years. Older, in fact, than De Gaulle, Nehru, and Khrushchev – all of whom are now close to age 80, and in much better shape.*

Justice: (*Hastily rechecking her records*) Mr. President, you do not – ah – look your age. Especially for an American.

**LBJ**: (*angry, but lacking energy to have an intimidating fit of temper*) Yeah, but at least I don't need a wheelchair. (*Glares at Churchill*)

**Churchill**: *The old bulldog rouses and growls back.* But at your age, I was leading Great Britain through its finest hour!

**LBJ** *calms down a bit and reaches for his cigarettes; then, remembering, looks longingly at them.* I gave these things up back when I had my first heart attack – that was when I was Senate Majority Leader. Followed the doctor's orders, lost weight and everything. I wasn't going to let anything stand in the way of becoming President and serving out my term. *He puts the cigarettes back in his pocket.* But right after Nixon's Inauguration, when we got on Air Force One back to Texas – as soon as the plane's door shut, I lit up. One of my girls scolded me, but I told her it was finally <u>my</u> time to do what I want!

**Justice**: So you indulged.

**LBJ**: Yep. Went back to 2-3 packs a day – and ate hamburgers, hamburgers, hamburgers. Someone made a pillow for our living room that says 'This is my ranch and I do as I damn well please.' And I did.

**R.A.Clio**: So you enjoyed Retirement?

**LBJ**: At first, yes. I left Washington after 32 years of working 20-hour days. I was dead tired, exhausted. I needed to be lazy for awhile. And it was a relief not to have to bother with people I didn't care about – or to deal with those snotty-nosed reporters. I figured I'd done my time with all of them. And I finally discovered how to play. (*Shakes his head*) That was a word that had never even been in my vocabulary.

<u>Recording Angel Clio</u>'s screen *shows* <u>LBJ</u> *on the beach in Mexico, hosting long dinners at his ranch, telling war stories about his years in politics, mimicking people he'd worked with. He is the center of attention, having a marvelous time, as are his guests.*

*The scene changes to Lyndon playing with his grandchildren, enjoying it immensely. He entertains them for hours with the same repetitive games, long after most adults would have lost patience.*

<u>R.A.Clio</u>: It looks like you're having fun. But surely this wasn't enough for a lifelong workaholic.

<u>LBJ</u>: (*nods in agreement*) True. But I had my ranch – which I loved more than anywhere on Earth. So I took charge, and ran it like I did my White House.

<u>Recording Angel</u>'s screen *shows Lyndon up at 6 AM, dogging the steps of the ranch manager and the ranch hands. 2-way radios are installed in every vehicle and all rooms, so he can reach anyone at any time. Nothing escapes his attention: the number of eggs laid, the state of fence repairs, the health of cattle, the irrigation of fields. There are Memos to the staff, meetings at which he exhorts them to 'make a solemn pledge not to go to bed tonight until you are sure that every steer has everything he needs!' And 'if we treat those hens with loving care, we can produce the finest eggs in the country.'*

<u>R.A.Clio</u>: And how did all that work out?

<u>LBJ</u>: Pretty well. Though cowboys aren't much good at writing memos. And the ranch manager kept wondering when I was going to run for President again.

<u>R.A.Clio</u>: You had a list of other projects, too?

LBJ: Yes. Of course, like most of you (*waves toward jury box*) I wrote my Memoirs. Though just of my Presidency. I wanted folks to know all I did. (*Pauses*) And you, too. *He looks hopefully at Clio.*

R.A.Clio: And how did that go?

LBJ: It was harder than I expected. I couldn't stand just sitting by myself writing, and dictating at a tape recorder was almost as bad. I felt cut off from people I could see and hear and get a response from. So I hired some smart folks to help. I got out my files, and we would talk about them – sort of like an interview.

R.A.Clio *flashes a scene of Lyndon speeding his convertible around the ranch, barking orders at his foreman, intermittently discussing his presidency with one of his writers, who is sitting in the back seat with an archives box on his lap, trying not to look scared.*

R.A.Clio: And these writers would then draft chapters?

LBJ: That was the idea. I wanted it to be Presidential, but they kept trying to slip in stories I'd told about people still in Washington. **(COLORFUL TEXAS PROFANITY)**, I couldn't say stuff like that. And I made them get rid of the street language. For **(more CTP)** sake, what did they think this was – the tale of an uneducated cowboy?! It's a presidential memoir, **(still more CTP)**, and I had to come out looking like a statesman – not some backwoods politician.

R.A.Clio: And the result?

LBJ: (*frowns*) Well... it was... presidential.

R.A.Clio (*turns to jury box*): Did any of you read it.

Nehru: I was already dead. (*Looks relieved*)

Khrushchev: I couldn't get books like that in exile. (*Grins*)

De Gaulle: (*trying to be diplomatic*) It was, indeed, presidential – but not at all like who you are.

Churchill: It sounds like the most bloody boring book every written! I'm glad I was dead and couldn't read it.

LBJ *reaches for his oxygen mask.*

R.A.Clio *changes the subject.* And what about your Museum and Library?

LBJ *hooks the mask back on the oxygen tank.* Now that turned out really well. It's all there – the story of my time – with the bark off. Any mistake, anything critical, ugly, unpleasant – all included. Papers from my years as President in one place for friend and foe to judge.

*He looks imploringly at Clio.* And I hope that you'll visit it some day, too.

R.A.Clio: I have already done so. And I compliment you for being so thorough. It is an honest – and very voluminous – archive.

LBJ: (*beaming*) Thank you, Ma'am. Thank you! I figure my reputation has nowhere to go but up.

R.A.Clio: Now tell us about the Public Affairs School.

LBJ: (*smiles again*) It was attached to the University of Texas in Austin. I did some fund-raising and started a generous endowment. And appointed some good people – with the right credentials – to teach and run it. I worried that the hands-on might get submerged by the academic and would have played a more active role making that not so – but Academia finally convinced me of its limits. *He shrugs.*

R.A.Clio: What else was on your list?

LBJ: Getting my financial affairs in order. I wanted to be sure that LadyBird and the girls wouldn't have to worry about that.

R.A.Clio: You started poor, but ended up quite wealthy.

LBJ: Yes, but I didn't really spend much time at it. I had a good head for business. Some people even said if I'd put as much energy into it as I did Public Service, I might have been the richest man on earth. (*Laughs*) But that wouldn't have been nearly as interesting as politics! And as President, I ended up doing much more good for folks than if I'd just given away money I'd probably gotten by cheating them.

R.A.Clio: And did all of this keep you busy enough?

LBJ: No. After a life like mine – how could it. (*Pauses*) Sometimes – when I got bored (*Chuckles*) I'd call some of my old cronies – and give them a bit of the Johnson Treatment on the phone. (*Laughs*) I could hear them sweating.

R.A.Clio: In fact, you died with a telephone in your hand, two days after that Term you didn't run for would have ended.

*On her screen,* Recording Angel Clio *shows* Walter Cronkite *broadcasting live about a cease-fire in Vietnam. Someone hands him a bulletin – 'Wait, this just in – former President Lyndon Johnson is dead.'*

153

*Screen then shows* <u>LBJ</u> *lying in state in his big new library/museum. The librarian is meticulously keeping track of how many people pay their respects. 'I know that somewhere, sometime, President Johnson's going to ask me.'*

<u>LBJ</u>: *(chuckles)* And someday I will. *(Chuckles again)* I got a state funeral in Washington, right? All Presidents get one of those.

<u>R.A.Clio</u>: You died a few days after Nixon's second Inauguration, so they just cancelled some of the events and transferred the personnel and arrangements to your funeral.

*Her screen shows* <u>LBJ</u> *lying in state in the Capitol Rotunda. Several friends keep watch all night. 'The thing Lyndon hated most,' LadyBird had told them, 'was to be by himself.'*

*Screen shifts to the large Washington church* <u>LBJ</u> *had attended. The usual dignitaries are present, and Leontyne Price sings 'Onward Christian Soldiers.' Finally a plane carries the body back to Texas, where it's interred in the family cemetery.*

<u>LBJ</u>: Well, kind of a boring funeral. No grieving mobs like some of you over there got. But at least there were no protestors.

<u>Khrushchev</u>: And at least you got one.

<u>LBJ</u>: True. *Hesitates.* Is there any stuff named after me – besides my Library and Public Affairs School?

<u>R.A.Clio</u>: Well, let's see. Ah, there's the LBJ Space Center in Houston... There's an LBJ National Grassland somewhere – and a Memorial Grove on the Potomac... There's an LBJ Runway at the Austin Airport and Interstate 635 in Dallas is the LBJ

Freeway. The U.S. Department of Education headquarters is named for you... And so is a Middle School in Florida.

*LBJ smiles briefly at the latter two, then looks disappointed.* Is that all?

*R.A.Clio nods.* But here's something to cheer you up.

*Screen shows LBJ lying in state in the Capitol Rotunda. The majority of those paying their respects are African Americans. A woman says to her little girl. 'Most people don't know it, but he did more for us than anybody.'*

LBJ: *(tears in his eyes).* I just wish I could have done more. *Silence. He hesitates, then looks at the* Recording Angel.

R.A.Clio: Yes?

*LBJ looks over at Khrushchev. Hesitates again. Finally asks very quietly:*

You were pretty nice to that fellow, Khrushchev. What are you going to say about me?

R.A.Clio: That's important to you, isn't it?

LBJ: H___, yes! I wanted to be as great a President as Lincoln – and FDR. But it seems like that damn war cast a big shadow over all my Great Society laws.

R.A.Clio: What do you think I should say?

*LBJ ponders.* Something like – I tried hard and did my best in very difficult times.

R.A.Clio: That's fair... But I can't just erase Vietnam.

LBJ *sighs.* Yes, I know. But please don't put me with all those forgotten Presidents – like Millard Fillmore or Chester Arthur. Or with the really dumb ones like Warren Harding.

R.A.Clio *smiles.* I assure you, that will never happen. And you, too, will never be forgotten.

*Fade out.*

# CHAPTER 9

# CLOSING ARGUMENTS

*Instead of being in the jury box, the players are sitting around a large round table.* Churchill *is at 12 o'clock and, moving clockwise,* De Gaulle *is next to him, then* Nehru, Khrushchev *and* LBJ.

De Gaulle *and* Nehru *are having a friendly conversation; in the course of the trial, they have discovered much in common.*

Khrushchev *and* LBJ *have made a similar discovery, but are sitting in uncomfortable silence, not quite knowing what to do with it.*

Churchill *is warily watching both these interactions, wondering what can be done to derail the connections.*

*All of them are once more in their prime.*

Justice: This trial has been concerned with determining your role in the Cold War. Each of you has been interrogated separately. Today, you will collectively discuss who is most to blame for starting – and continuing – it.

R.A.Clio: All of you were powerful leaders of large nations. How did the Cold War affect your country?

Khrushchev: After the devastation of the Great Patriotic War, we had to rebuild what had been destroyed. But we were encircled by hostile powers. So we had to maintain large armed forces and build nuclear weapons to discourage incursions into our buffer zones. There wasn't much left over for making life more comfortable for the people. They had sacrificed so much for so long – they deserved a reward. I wanted to make things better for my folks, too. *He looks meaningfully at* LBJ. But the Cold War got in the way.

LBJ: We never had to choose between guns and butter. In fact, making the guns seemed to keep the economy going so there would be more butter. The Cold War kept demanding more guns, so there was no shortage of 'butter.' President Eisenhower warned us of the danger of the Military-Industrial Complex, but it seemed necessary to contain Communism and defend our way of life. All of the resulting armed conflicts were fought somewhere else, and usually didn't bother most Americans. But I think there were meanwhile problems that got neglected. I tried to fix them, but the Vietnam War got in the way.

Nehru: Like other 3rd World countries, India was too often caught in the crossfire between the superpowers. You Americans, especially, demanded that we choose sides. We needed help from everywhere, but when the Soviets helped us build steel mills and dams, you branded us as Communists – and sent arms to Pakistan. Which forced us to divert much needed resources to building defensive armed forces. India has never had enough 'butter' – millions starve every year. Instead of money and resources being wasted on lethal weapons, it should have been used to help underdeveloped nations like India develop.

De Gaulle: Europe was in the middle of you superpowers, and was the main area of contention. My country had been devastated by too many wars too often, so I had to protect her. I could not let France be a pawn in the East-West struggle. So I allied with West Germany, and together we constructed the European Union as a counterforce in the Cold War. And so that France would be treated with proper respect, we developed our own nuclear weapons!

Churchill: The British Empire was worn out by World War II. To maintain our existence, we needed a strong alliance with the Americans. But they were all too ready to retreat again into isolationism. They needed another enemy we could fight together. Communism threatened everything that I, as an aristocrat, valued and was undermining the Empire. So I urged the Americans to recognize the danger. And also to share their nuclear weapons with us.

Justice: Thank you, Gentlemen. After listening to the previous testimony and seeing all the evidence, who do you consider most to blame for the Cold War?

Let's begin with General De Gaulle.

De Gaulle: The opening round of the Cold War had to do with the Soviets re-acquiring traditional buffer zones. You Americans saw this as a repeat of Appeasing Hitler. But after what happened to Russia during the two world wars, can anyone doubt that the Tsars would have settled the frontiers and territory any differently than Stalin did?

*Looks over at* Churchill *and frowns.*

The Americans are notoriously ignorant of anyone's history – even their own – but you, Sir Winston, should have known better!

Churchill: And you should have tried to get along with FDR. I made several efforts to build a bridge between you.

De Gaulle: He was very unfriendly.

Churchill: Nonsense! Meeting him was like opening your first bottle of champagne.

De Gaulle: I dislike champagne.

Churchill: Bah! Your problem is that you think you're Joan of Arc.

De Gaulle: And your problem is that your bishops wouldn't let you burn me.

*He returns to his narrative.*

When Stalin died, the Soviet Union became much easier to deal with – mainly due to your efforts, Comrade Khrushchev, to open up and lead your country toward détente.

*Looks at* Khrushchev, *who smiles.*

Unlike Stalin's menacing inscrutability, your jovial and spontaneous personality did not alarm. But, Nikita Sergeevich, your quirkish behavior sometimes made communication difficult.

Khrushchev *looks surprised.*

At that disastrous Paris summit, you really should have made up with President Eisenhower about the U-2 incident! I offered you both several opportunities for rapprochement.

*His frown silences* Khrushchev's *protest.*

De Gaulle *continues.* Eisenhower, too, was in a difficult political position at home. While he understood the situation of the Russians after the war – he, too, was there – America was in the midst of a vicious anti-communist hysteria.

*He looks at* LBJ.

You Americans need to adopt a more realistic attitude toward Communists in general. I myself regarded them as potentially troublesome, but recognized their courageous role in the Resistance, and could never therefore deny the Communist Party a place in my government. They were, in fact, less trouble than your NATO forces.

LBJ *looks surprised.*

De Gaulle *frowns.* NATO was supposed to be a cooperative alliance, but you Americans bossed everyone around. And your arrogance put France at risk. Someone had to show you that this was not acceptable. And so, among other things, we French built our own Bomb. At the time it seemed a good idea. In retrospect, I regret it. Though ours was but a small part of the total nuclear arsenal – it still added to the overall problem.

De Gaulle *shakes his head, then looks regretfully at* LBJ.

But your biggest mistake as President was repeating one of our worst mistakes. We warned you about Vietnam. But as Voltaire said, 'Those who are ignorant of History are doomed to repeat it.' That War almost destroyed an entire Asian country, and escalated the Cold War to even more obscene heights. Ho Chi Minh was <u>not</u> a puppet of the Chinese Communists. On the contrary. Before we French took over his country, the Chinese Emperors had ruled it for 1000 years. In the wake of the Japanese defeat in WWII, the Chinese returned – this time calling themselves Nationalists. Ho allied with us to drive them out. He knew that if they stayed this time, they would never leave. So when Mao's Communists took over China, it made little difference to Ho Chi Minh. They were still Chinese. The Vietnamese wanted their own country. They were fighting for their Independence – as were colonies all over the world. As did you Americans back in the day. You should have helped – like the Russians did.

<u>De Gaulle</u> *turns to* <u>Churchill</u>. And you should have let go of your Empire – like France eventually did – instead of clinging to it.

<u>De Gaulle</u> *looks again at* <u>Justice</u> *and resumes his statement.*
Meanwhile, I did what I could to mediate disputes. Paris was the site of many Summit Conferences – some more successful than others.

*He shoots a disapproving glance at* <u>Khrushchev</u>.

And I made peace with the German Enemy next door. Adenauer and I forged the European Union as a third force to balance the superpowers. Just as Prime Minister Nehru did in Asia.

*He nods approvingly at* <u>Nehru</u>.

<u>De Gaulle</u> *concludes.* Those were difficult times. My first allegiance was to France, so that she could be a positive balance in the world. For only then could France – and all of us –be safe.

Justice: Prime Minister Nehru, you're next. Where do you think blame lies for the Cold War?

Nehru *looks around the table at his peers, struggling to regard* Churchill *in a Gandhian fashion.*

When you British finally departed, you left the railroads you'd built for the purpose of exploiting us more efficiently. But no other industrial infrastructure had been needed to do that – so there was none. This was how colonies were customarily treated. And although some of your colleagues were more enlightened, your own way of dealing with colonies who desired independence was to send in troops to suppress it.

But worst of all, was how you encouraged Jinnah and the Moslim League – and allowed them to strengthen their movement while we were all locked up in your jails. The greatest curse of India is the Partition and creation of Pakistan. Without that constant running sore, one of the continuous conflicts fueling the Cold War could have been eliminated.

Nehru *pauses to regain his composure, then continues, smiling at* De Gaulle.

Like you, we tried to be a force for peace. Like you, we created a third force – of Asian unaligned nations – as a balance between the U.S. and U.S.S.R. I, too, mediated international disputes when I could, and often served as an unofficial messenger in world diplomacy.

And we tried to be good neighbors. Non-recognition of Red China was as ridiculous as non-recognition of the Soviet Union long after its Revolution was a fait accompli. So we were among the first to recognize Mao's new government, and I worked hard to build cordial relations between India and China. At first, I was successful – or thought I was. But dealing with the Chinese can be... tricky.

*He looks meaningfully at* <u>Khrushchev</u>, *who nods ruefully.*

Russia was always a good neighbor.

*He smiles at* <u>Khrushchev</u>, *and does a grateful and prolonged 'namaste'.*

You helped us build our much needed infrastructure, without which we could never have become economically independent. Your technical advisors, sent to oversee the construction of steel mills and dams, brought their families and stayed awhile. They worked as equals with our technicians, and our families made good friends with their families. In doing this, I knew that you were staying true to your ideals that good Communists should help emerging colonies develop. You Americans (*looks at* <u>LBJ</u>) always misunderstood such aid as 'Communist Aggression.' But I <u>know</u> firsthand how bad colonialism is – and how much we needed help such as our Russian neighbors gave.

That said, Nikita Sergeevich, (*looks at* <u>Khrushchev</u>) I do think that sending your Missiles to Cuba was unwise – and stretched that policy of aid too thin.

<u>Nehru</u> *politely addresses* <u>LBJ</u>.
Mr. President, allow me to thank you for shipping your surplus grain to us in times of famine. It is typical of American generosity. Unfortunately, Americans are also prone to lecturing other countries about how they should run their affairs. I'm sure you meant well when you admonished us to work hard and pull ourselves up by our bootstraps. But Mr. President, India is not Texas.

India does not tell her neighbors what to do at home. And we value the study of History – our own, and everyone else's. *Salutes R.A.Clio.* Had you learned this from us, you might have avoided the tragedy of Vietnam. *He shakes his head sadly.* So many lives lost, so many resources wasted that could have been used to help them build an independent country.

And one more thing. *His formidable but usually controlled temper flairs.* All those high-tech weapons you sent to Pakistan: Have you any idea how much devastating havoc you caused in India – and Pakistan? How much this strained our already inadequate military resources? How incredibly short-sighted such a policy was?! Pakistan might even have rejoined us without that support.

Nehru, *trembling with indignation, glares at* LBJ. Khrushchev *puts a friendly but restraining hand on his shoulder.* Recording Angel Clio *quickly intervenes and whispers in* Nehru's *ear. He calms down and smiles ironically.*

I'm told that all these weapons eventually bit the U.S.A. in the butt – big-time!

*He shakes his head.*

But that is small comfort.

*After a brief recess to allow everyone to calm down,* Justice *recalls the Court to order.*

Comrade Khrushchev, it's your turn.

Khrushchev: Because we have no naturally defensible barriers, we have been constantly invaded. Our main defense is to surround our heartland with buffer zones. And then to be strong enough to discourage attack. Or at least to look strong. Which we weren't by the end of the Great Patriotic War. We had fought so hard and lost so much, we were exhausted. Rebuilding all that the Germans had destroyed was our first priority. There was nothing left over to be aggressive with. Moving into territory on our Western border was not aggression. Those areas have been tossed around for centuries between anyone strong enough to claim them. And besides, since they were on the path to Berlin, we were already there.

*He faces* <u>LBJ</u>. So your fears of us taking over the world were unfounded.

<u>Churchill</u>: Russia is a riddle wrapped in a mystery inside an enigma. But Communism is an evil menace that must be destroyed everywhere!

<u>Khrushchev</u>: No! That's what Capitalism is! But we must somehow coexist! You should not have passed on your rabid anti-Communism to the Americans!

<u>LBJ</u>: But you Communists were taking over places like China and Laos and Vietnam. And what about all those Berlin crises?

<u>Khrushchev</u>: Not all Communists are the same. Red China worried us, too – especially since we share a long, long border. As for the Berlin Wall, that was mainly the doing of the East Germans.

*He looks at* <u>Churchill</u>.
And what idiot put West Berlin in the middle of East Germany!

<u>Khrushchev</u> *continues*. Now, I do admit that starting the missile race was my fault. At the time, it seemed like a good way to decrease our armies. I should have realized that you Americans would take the idea and run with it. And then Brezhnev thought

he had to match you. *He shakes his head.* But even then, all we wanted was parity. You Americans kept escalating to get superiority. And we couldn't just disarm, because by that time we were encircled by the forces of Western imperialism.

*He faces* De Gaulle. And yes, you're right. I should have calmed down at that Paris Summit. Instead, we lost a real chance to end the insanity of missile overkill. But I felt so betrayed by Eisenhower... If only we'd had the hotline then.

*He turns to* Nehru. And yes, putting missiles in Cuba probably wasn't wise. But the Americans needed to know how it felt to have enemy missiles in their backyard. And Yankee Imperialism in Latin America was the really greedy aggressive kind of Capitalism. Castro's outpost had to be defended. Still, we came much too close to disaster. But at least after that, we had a hotline between the Kremlin and the White House.

LBJ: But if all your actions were defensive, why did you threaten to bury us?

Khrushchev *sighs.* If only there had been even a few people in Washington who understood Russian! *Sighs again.* The word I used did not mean we would literally destroy and bury you, but that we would survive and be present at your funeral. Capitalism is based on greed and inequality. Any country enslaved by it will someday collapse under its own evil weight. Just like Marx said. But we shall endure.

Justice: Mr. President? Your turn.

LBJ, *genuinely puzzled, addresses* Khrushchev.
I don't understand why you thought you were encircled.

Khrushchev: Just look at the Map.

<u>Recording Angel's</u> *screen shows the usual U.S. – U.S.S.R. side by side map, with an 'iron curtain' dividing East and West.*

<u>LBJ</u>: I don't see it.

<u>Khrushchev</u>: That's because you aren't looking from the right perspective.

<u>Recording Angel</u> *switches maps to a global view from the top down. With the North Pole as reference point, one sees that Russia is indeed surrounded by U.S. territory or U.S. allies and friendlies, many of which host U.S. army/navy bases and/or missile installations pointed at Russia.*

<u>LBJ</u>: (*dumbfounded*) Hmmm... Well... All of that was to contain <u>your</u> aggression. We truly believed that you were a threat to our way of life. How were we to know otherwise? You were so secretive and Stalin – well, he was a brutal S.O.B. – even you thought so! You Commies were popping up all over the globe, fomenting revolutions everywhere. You all seemed alike, and we assumed you were all working together. We wanted to spare weak countries from being enslaved and help them learn the blessings of democracy and the American Way.

<u>Khrushchev</u>: And <u>we</u> wanted to protect them from the evils of Capitalism.

<u>LBJ</u>: What evils? We have freedom and democracy.

<u>Khrushchev</u>: What about equality?

<u>LBJ</u> *hesitates.* Well – we're working on that. But what about freedom in <u>your</u> territory?

<u>Khrushchev</u> *hesitates.* Well – we're working on that.

168

*Both are silent, thinking hard.*

Nehru: If I may intrude for just a moment. It occurs to me that you both see the world through different lenses. Perhaps you should widen your world view.

LBJ: What the h___ is a world view? We have two big oceans – East and West – and weak neighbors North and South. That protects us from a world that most of our grandparents crossed those oceans to get away from. And the first thing they did was to lose the foreign languages and speak American. And become American. That's how we view the world.

Nehru: But not everyone sees it like that.

LBJ: Why the h___ not? It's the best way. Who wouldn't want to live like Americans?

Nehru: Ho Chi Minh

LBJ: But he was a Communist!

Nehru: Because he thought it was the best way to liberate his country.

LBJ: He was wrong!

Nehru: He thought you were wrong, because he viewed the world differently.

Khrushchev: As do I. My world view is that of Marx and Lenin – which is the best way. But I know that many people don't agree. So my world is bigger than yours. Which gives me an edge.

<u>LBJ</u> *looks confused.*

<u>Nehru</u>: Perhaps you are <u>both</u> right – <u>and</u> wrong.

<u>LBJ</u> and <u>Khrushchev</u> *both look confused.*

*After another recess, during which both* <u>LBJ</u> *and* <u>Khrushchev</u> *eye each other quizzically,* <u>Justice</u> *calls the Court to order.*

And finally, Sir Winston, what have you to say about the Cold War?

<u>Churchill</u> *takes command of the table with the superior air of a British aristocrat. He speaks with that British accent which unfailingly convinces people that he not only knows what he's talking about – but that he is* <u>*right!*</u>

Bah! You're all wrong. The only world view worth considering is that of the British Empire. The Pax Britannica kept the peace all during the 19$^{th}$ Century. Unfortunately after two big wars we could no longer do it by ourselves. So we made the Americans our junior partner. Their big corporations, who had already copied some of our colonial practices, were very pleased by this. But to keep their government fully engaged we had to convince them that Soviet Russia was a threat to their security. This, of course, was balance of power politics as usual. Our role has always been to prevent anyone from challenging our supremacy by encouraging a counter-threat. Russia had become too powerful, so we positioned the U.S. to balance the threat. The Cold War was an expected result, and helped us maintain our Empire. The best hope for world peace is for a joint Pax of the English-speaking peoples. So I don't see what all the fuss is about!

**LBJ**: *More than a little cowed by the British accent, he speaks less assertively than usual.* We saved your a__ twice! So we're no one's junior partner!

Nehru *looks at* LBJ *sympathetically.* It's hard to resist, isn't it. That 'proper accent' is such wonderful propaganda for the glories of their Empire. But even though I know the dark side of their imperialism, I must battle to resist forgetting how brutal they can be. And that their Empire has done more harm than good. Most of the flashpoints in the Cold War were in colonies fighting for independence. The British had more colonies than anyone, so...

De Gaulle: It was easier for us to give up our Empire because its center was France, which did not need colonies to be France. The Empire is England – so without colonies what is England?

Khrushchev: England is Imperialism – the kind Marx predicted would eventually dig its own grave. *He grins at* Churchill *in an unfriendly fashion.* We shall bury you, too!

Churchill *is totally unfazed by the comments of his peers, completely convinced of his own superior rectitude.*
And what do you propose to keep the world from destroying itself?

The United Nations? The Soviet Union? The United States? The European Union?

The British Commonwealth is still the largest Coalition in the world, and its members are all over the globe. This is what England is!

Justice: Perhaps so. But couldn't this have happened without all the suffering and devastation of the Cold War?

# CHAPTER 10

# THE VERDICT

Justice: Here in Purgatory, we believe that the Punishment should suit the Crime, that the penance should fit the sinner, and that Goodness merits more than just being its own reward. Each of you will therefore be given a custom-tailored sentence. To ensure a proper fit, we need to know beforehand what heaven – and hell – would be to each of you.

*Laughter and groans, wry and witty comments from various occupants of the jury box.*

Justice: Mr. Nehru, let's start with you. What, for you, would be Heaven?

Nehru: That's the easiest question you've asked me. My life has been full of so many good experiences that I have only to choose my favorite circumstances. *He ponders briefly.* Heaven for me would be living back in Anand Bhawan, with my family – expecially my father and little sisters. I would have what was always my room, with desk and shelves full of good books. The house itself would, as usual, be full of guests. Gandhiji and other freedom fighters with whom I went to jail would be frequent

172

visitors. There would be beautiful and lively children with whom to play, beautiful and intelligent women with whom to converse. And none of us would ever go to jail again.

Justice: And what of India?

Nehru: India would be as we hoped, full of schools and hospitals – and no starving people. And India would be WHOLE. Unpartitioned, with no Pakistan to constantly be at war with. *Pauses.* I would no longer be in charge. The government would be in the hands of capable successors – preferably not of a Nehru dynasty. I might occasionally represent India at meetings of the Commonwealth and the United Nations. I would have an active correspondence with all the interesting people I met in my life. And I would very much love to have time to write my Memoirs.

Justice: And what, for you, would be Hell?

Nehru: (*without hesitating*) Living in India under the Raj, being condescended to by Englishmen convinced of their superiority and righteousness. Being in English jails. Having to relive the upheavals of the Partition. *Ponders.* And yes, living too long and losing my mind to dementia. *Hesitates.*

Justice: Yes?

Nehru: Wherever you send me, PLEASE let there be no one speaking in that accent. You know the one I mean.

*Everyone in the Courtroom (except Churchill) nods.*

Justice: General De Gaulle is next. S'il vous plait, Monsieur le General, qu'est-ce que c'est Heaven?

De Gaulle: Ah, oui. Ce n'est pas difficile! France as she should be. Democratic but with an orderly uncontentious Parlement, composed of considerably fewer than the usual multitude of political parties. The President would have sufficient power without being a dictator; there would be no need for a man on horseback. The European Union would be doing well, playing its intended balancing role between East and West.

Justice: And what of your personal life?

De Gaulle: I would live at Columbey, with a Jesuit priest in the local church.

Justice: Come now, General, that's not very personal. We're talking about all eternity here. Surely just this once you can unbend your military bearing?

De Gaulle *hesitates, then speaks very softly.* And I would like the company of my dear child, Anne, who died much too soon.

*He pauses, remembering his youngest child. The screen flashes a memory of little Anne, who has Downs syndrome, running to meet him at the door. Her smile lights up her entire body, as she joyfully holds out her arms. He unbends his very tall body, kneels down to her level, and returns her enthusiastic hug with infinite tenderness. Later, when they go out for a walk, he carefully wraps his scarf around her head and gently takes her hand. Only with her does he smile whole-heartedly.*

De Gaulle *returns to his description of heaven.*
...There would be occasional visits to Paris, consulting with those government officials desiring my wisdom. I would correspond actively with the various world leaders I've met. Monsieur Nehru, I would especially like to know you better. And – oh yes – I would like to finish my Memoirs.

Justice: And what about Hell?

De Gaulle: (*without hesitating*) To be locked in with the French Chamber of Deputies, as it usually is. Especially during the 1930s, with its constant cabinet crises and Maginot Psychology. And... *hesitates...* to live in Texas. *Looks at* LBJ. Pardonnez-moi, Monsieur le President, but Americans speak French with atrocious accents. Even to imagine the Texas version is unbearable.

LBJ: No one in Texas wants to speak French, so it wouldn't be a problem.

De Gaulle: Ah, but no French at all would be even worse. Though not as bad as living in Vichy France, where even singing 'La Marseillaise' was forbidden.

Justice: Anything else?

De Gaulle: Well... wherever you send me, please don't make me dance.

*Looking as close as he ever gets to appearing embarrassed, he returns to his seat.*

Justice: Comrade Khrushchev, you're next.

Khrushchev: I still think Heaven probably doesn't exist. Anyway, it will be unnecessary when the Soviet Union fulfills its destiny as a truly Communist Country. There will be a classless society – from each according to their abilities, to each according to their needs. Capitalism will dig its own grave and colonialism disappear, so there will be no need for armies and bombs and missiles. At last there will be enough for everyone to live decently. This is what I worked for all my life. We all did. Even

175

Stalin, before capitalist encirclement pushed him into seeing enemies everywhere.

Justice: And what of your private circumstances?

Khrushchev: In a truly Socialist society, public space is more important – and available – than private space. The small dacha I had in retirement, minus the KGB guards, would be sufficient. Perhaps a bigger yard, so I could grow some corn, have a dog, and keep a few interesting pets for my grandchildren. Mostly, though, I would want something to do. Wouldn't need – or want – to be boss again – just to be useful. And I really wish Russians could read my Memoirs.

Justice: And what of Hell?

Khrushchev *laughs*. My whole life has been Hell! Oh, not just the hard work and constant destruction, civil war and foreign invasions. No, that's just life as usual in Russia. What's Hell is being in charge of a country whose geography is overwhelming and where almost all the choices are bad. And meanwhile, no one elsewhere bothers to look at a map and understand.

Justice: What about being sent to a Gulag?

Khrushchev: Yes, that would be fair. But for most of us, most of the time, life was not that much better, so...

Justice: Anything else?

Khrushchev: (*smiles at* De Gaulle) Unlike the General, I like to dance.

(*Winks at* Nehru) And since I don't speak English the accent is not a problem.

But please, PLEASE don't send me to another of Stalin's drunken feasts!

Justice: President Johnson, your turn. What's your idea of Heaven?

LBJ: First of all, I wouldn't be President. I'd be Senate Majority Leader again, making deals and getting consensus, making things better for folks and implementing all those Great Society laws I'd already passed. There would always be plenty of hands to shake – and some arms to twist. But I'd make the day longer so I could spend more time at my ranch, playing with my grandkids – and making up all the time I didn't spend with my daughters. *Pauses.* The Vietnam War would NEVER have happened. *Pauses again.* And there would be no Kennedys.

Justice: And what about Hell?

LBJ: Obviously, ANYTHING to do with that mess in Vietnam. To have to relive all those agonizing doubts and decisions and frustrations. To have all that power – and yet feel powerless to do anything right. And worrying about all those American boys getting killed.

Justice: What about all the Vietnamese people?

LBJ: *(almost at a loss for words)* I couldn't – can't – let myself go there... The load on our side was about as much as I could bear.

Justice: And on the personal front, what would your Hell be?

LBJ: *(quietly and without hesitation)* To be alone. No folks to talk to, no hands to shake, no deals to be made... And no LadyBird.

<u>Justice</u>: She's already in Heaven, being amply rewarded for putting up with you.

<u>LBJ</u> s*miles hugely.* OK, now make sure everyone treats her right. A lot of people didn't appreciate what a great lady she was. Bird <u>never</u> let me down.

<u>Justice</u>: Anything else?

<u>LBJ</u>: Yeah. I sure hope you don't send me to Hell – cause I really don't want to meet Bobby Kennedy again. But wherever I go... *He grins at* <u>De Gaulle</u> *in a not unfriendly fashion....* Please don't make me speak French!

<u>Justice</u>: And finally, Sir Winston, it's your turn.

<u>Churchill</u> *is wearing his 'siren suit'. One can almost hear the air raid alerts wailing.*

<u>Justice</u>: Interesting attire, Sir Winston.

<u>Churchill</u>: *(grinning cherubically)* Yes, I designed it myself. Whenever the sirens went off, all I had to do was pull on my jumpsuit and zip it up. And out I would go to shake my fist at Hitler's bombs.

<u>Justice</u>: What if one had landed on your head?

<u>Churchill</u>: Bah! That bloodthirsty guttersnipe wouldn't have dared!

<u>Justice</u> *laughs.* I see. Now tell us about your personal Heaven.

<u>Churchill</u>: For most of my life, I <u>was</u> in Heaven, living in the British Empire. Especially before World War I, it was the best

of all possible places. And I was a member of the best of all possible classes, and the best of all possible races. I could go almost anywhere in the world and be recognized as such. I hunted rhinoceros in Africa, and rode in the last real cavalry charge. As a soldier I saw action on four continents. One could find adventure everywhere, exploring the depths of mysterious territory and expanding the limits of the Empire.

Justice: And what of the people already there?

Churchill: Sometimes they had to be convinced to accept the gifts of civilization offered by the British Empire.

Nehru *cannot suppress a snort of indignation.*

Churchill *cannot suppress a scowl in return.*

One could always find a good fight somewhere. And then write a best-selling book about it. And since native weaponry was usually inferior, one was rarely in any real danger. Nothing in life is so exhilarating as to be shot at without result.

Justice: So the Empire was a huge playground for you?

Churchill *tries to resist, but is compelled to tell the truth.* Well... yes. But all of this was to serve the world by means of the Pax Britannica.

Justice: Besides being Prime Minister, how did you, specifically, serve?

Churchill: I was in the House of Commons for years, and held several Cabinet posts before becoming Prime Minister. My favorite was as First Lord of the Admiralty. The British Navy was truly a wonder to behold – and to command!

<u>Justice</u>: The best of all possible toys?

<u>Churchill</u> *struggles to deny, but instead growls quietly.*

<u>Justice</u>: What about Gallipoli and the Dardanelles?

<u>Churchill</u> *groans.* Even thinking about that disastrous battle is <u>my</u> idea of Hell. One of the worst British naval defeats ever! And it was on <u>my</u> watch.

<u>Justice</u>: And what else is Hell for you?

<u>Churchill</u>: NOT to be British. And for there to be NO Empire... That would be Hell for everyone.

*Recess*

<u>Justice</u>: Thank you, gentlemen. And now we shall see how your lives weigh in on the Scales of History, and what your resulting fate shall be.

<u>Recording Angel:</u> Here in Purgatory, we don't deal in terms of black and white. For politicians that would clearly be both unjust – and impossible. What we do instead, is to consider the environment from which you emerged, the problems your country faced, and what you did to solve them. The resources available and obstacles to be overcome will, of course, be factored in. And although the main issue on which you are being judged is your role in the Cold War, we recognize that your domestic policies are also relevant to why things happened as they did.

All of you made mistakes. But the bottom line here is the overall balance. Did the good outweigh the bad? Or did the harm you caused overwhelm whatever benefits you sought to bestow.

<u>Justice</u>: The Court of Purgatory calls Prime Minister Nehru of India to be judged for his role in the Cold War.

<u>Nehru</u> rises and faces the <u>Recording Angel</u>.

*The Scale of Justice has become huge.*

<u>R.A.Clio</u> *stands behind its two shallow pans, which are hanging by slender chains on opposite ends of the balance beam. On one side is a large bowl of light marbles, on the other a bowl of dark marbles.*

<u>R.A.Clio</u> *reads from the Book of History:*
Jawaharlal Nehru: you were born into wealth and could easily have stayed in your comfortable niche and, as an only son, become a spoiled brat. Instead, you voluntarily gave all that up to become a leader of your people. Your dedication to non-violence, your years in jail, your skillful organization and negotiation in the cause of Independence for India are duly noted.

*She puts several light marbles in the Right Pan.*

As Prime Minister for the rest of your life, you forged India's innumerable religions and cultures and languages into a nation. You endeavored to alleviate crushing poverty by building countless schools and hospitals, and by constructing steel-mills and factories to enable India's economic independence.

*She puts more light marbles in the Right Pan.*

Meanwhile, you brought together other developing Asian nations into an Association of Non-aligned States to provide a neutral counterbalance to the East and West. And you often mediated to reduce conflict.

*More light marbles.*

Throughout your tenure, you maintained a balance between Socialism and Democracy. And won a reputation for absolute integrity. Even critics agreed that your honesty was unassailable.

*Still more light marbles.*

For 17 years, you had enough power to have easily become king or emperor or whatever kind of autocrat you chose. But you never became a dictator or tyrant.

*She empties the bowl of light marbles onto the already loaded pan. It crashes to the floor; several marbles spill over and roll out.*

<u>R.A.Clio</u> *indicates the still full bowl of dark marbles, and turns the page.*
On the other hand, there were some serious sins of omission. While you were raising the standard of living with your hospitals and schools, India became even more overpopulated. Your population control policies were too little, too late.

*She puts dark marbles into the Wrong Pan. The other Pan does not budge.*

And while you were building infrastructure for heavy industry, you neglected cottage industries in the villages.

*More dark marbles. Still no movement.*

As for the Partition, you failed to understand the appeal of Jinnah and his Muslim League. And after Partition, it would have been wiser to allow Kashmir to become independent. Even if Pakistan had immediately moved in, it would have removed the principal battleground between your countries – and perhaps eliminated a prime training ground for jihadists.

*A big handful of dark marbles are added to the Wrong Pan. The connecting chains of the Right Pan straighten.*

And finally, you allowed your personal friendship with Zhou En Lai to cloud your judgment. When the Chinese invaded, India's troops were unprepared. There were too many unnecessary casualties.

*Another handful of dark marbles into the Wrong Pan. The Right Pan of light marbles finally lifts a few centimeters. The bowl of dark marbles is still more than half full.*

R.A.Clio: The Verdict is clear. The Right outweighs the Wrong, especially since most of your mistakes were sins of omission rather than sins of commission. India was in chaos. It is amazing that you accomplished as much as you did.

*She picks up some of the light marbles which have spilled on the floor and adds them to the Right Pan, which lowers back to the floor.*

Justice: Your Sentence, Jawaharlal Nehru, is to live in the heaven of your choice at Anand Bhawan, reading those few books you have not yet read – and writing your Memoirs. You are also to be a member of God's Cabinet, and to be Heaven's representative to the United Nations.

Nehru *smiles and does 'namaste' all around.*

Justice: You will enjoy your conversations with God. S/He is beautiful and very intelligent.

*A brief Recess*

Justice: The Court of Purgatory calls General Charles De Gaulle, President of the French Republic, to be judged for his role in the Cold War.

<u>De Gaulle</u> *as always, stands at attention before* Justice.

R.A.Clio *has put all the marbles back in their respective bowls. Standing behind the Scales of History, she turns the page to De Gaulle's record.*

When the French gave up and allowed the Nazi occupation and the puppet Vichy regime, you carried the fight to the French Colonies, gained their support for Fighting France, and organized their troops to join the war effort. Though not as large as the British Empire, the French Empire was as widely dispersed around the globe. Getting to these places was not easy, especially since transportation usually depended on persuading the British to provide passage on their planes and ships. Your only resource was your passion to liberate France, yet you single-handedly rallied your colonies to the cause.

*She places several light marbles in the Right Pan.*

Meanwhile, you organized the Resistance in occupied France, which greatly facilitated the Normandy Invasion. You also gathered a regiment of regular French troops and persuaded Eisenhower to let them liberate Paris.

*Many more light marbles.*

You saved France from the Nazis, and from being erased by the Allies. Then you made order out of the chaos left behind, and put France back together.

*More light marbles.*

During your later term as President, you often mediated between East and West, and hosted Summit conferences.

*More light marbles. The Right Pan is almost touching the floor.*

You let the French Empire go, and allowed the colonies to be independent.

*More light marbles. The Right Pan is resting on the floor.*

You persuaded Adenauer's West Germany to help you start the European Union as a balancing force to the Superpowers.

*More light marbles. The Right Pan is almost full.*

Although you sometimes assumed dictatorial powers to do what was needed, you always returned them when the crisis passed. And when your effectiveness as a leader diminished, you voluntarily resigned.

*More light marbles. The Right Pan is full, though not spilling over. The bowl of light marbles is not quite empty.*

<u>R.A.Clio</u> *turns the page to his negative record.*
On the other hand, your zeal to protect France caused you to be difficult to work with. Especially during the War, you could have asserted France's Honor with less hauteur. And you should have made use of Churchill's attempts to build a bridge between you and FDR, especially after you had proved that France was you – not Vichy.

*She puts some dark marbles in the Wrong Pan.*

And after the War, you would have been more successful in reducing American hubris had you also shown gratitude for their liberation of France from the Nazis.

*More dark marbles in the Wrong Pan. The slack chains on the Right Pan straighten.*

In your zeal to protect France, did you sometimes allow the line between her honor and your ego to blur?

*More dark marbles.*

You often made use of France to mediate and defuse the Cold War. But France is not what she used to be. Perhaps it is time to let her act her age.

<u>De Gaulle</u> *is obviously not pleased by what he perceives as an insult to France. With difficulty he maintains his military bearing.*

<u>R.A.Clio</u> *puts more dark marbles in the Wrong Pan, still swinging above the floor. The bowl next to it is more than half full. The chains of both Pans are straight, but the Right Pan is firmly resting on the floor.*

The verdict is clear. The Right outweighs the Wrong. Despite personal sacrifice and danger, you stayed true to the Path of Honor – and led others to follow. You accepted the role of temporary autocrat when France needed one, and then returned power to the people without need of a Revolution. This is remarkable, especially in French History.

<u>Justice</u>: You are sentenced to the Heaven of your choice: living simply at Colombey – and yes, little Anne will be there, too. Please do finish your Memoirs. You are a marvelous writer, and remarkably honest about what you remember.

*Looks at* <u>Clio</u>. Give him some more light marbles for that.

<u>R.A.Clio</u> *nods and complies.*

<u>Justice</u>: You will also have a charming little room, in a typical Paris hotel, to use when you are called as an emergency advisor to the French government.

God also wants you to work with NATO. It needs to be turned into an Alliance against Terrorism. Try to persuade them to get the Russians to join.

*Pauses.* But no. You will not be joining God's Cabinet. S/He is not French.

*Brief Recess*

<u>Justice</u>: The Court now calls Nikita Khrushchev, Premier of the Soviet Union.

<u>R.A.Clio</u>: As a Commissar during World War II, you were on the front lines during several crucial battles, and actively participated in liberating your country from the Nazis.

*She places several light marbles in the Right Pan.*

But you took much longer to liberate your people from Stalin. You were part of his inner circle, and shared in the adulation which elevated him to absolute power.

*Several dark marbles in the Wrong Pan.*

And as Boss of the Ukraine, you followed orders and sent countless innocent people to the Gulag.

*Many dark marbles in the Wrong Pan.*

However, you eventually realized your error, and publicly admitted it. Hundreds of thousands of innocent prisoners were released.

*Many light marbles in the Right Pan.*

In denouncing Stalin and travelling to the U.S., you presented the world with a much less menacing image of the USSR. This reduced East-West tension and enabled better communication.

*More light marbles.*

But it was you who initiated the missile race by claiming many more than you actually had.

*Dark marbles.*

But you did this in order to reduce your armies and divert resources to improve living conditions for your people, who had sacrificed too much for too long.

*Light marbles.*

You and Eisenhower allowed the U-2 incident to sabotage the Paris Summit. An opportunity to end the Cold War was thereby lost.

*Dark marbles.*

You sent technical aid to developing countries like India, and helped them build necessary steel-mills and dams.

*Light marbles.*

You tried to send missiles to Cuba, which precipitated a crisis which came perilously close to World War III.

*Handful of dark marbles.*

But you wisely backed off, made a deal with Kennedy, and the hotline between capitols was set up.

*Light marbles.*

You lessened censorship in Russia, and opened up to cultural exchange visits with the U.S.

*Light marbles.*

*Both Pans are now hanging in the air, but the Wrong Pan is weighing somewhat heavier.*

Justice: Comrade Khrushchev, although the Wrongs appear to outweigh the Rights, the Court takes into account the sincerity of your intentions and your dedication to a potentially just system. It also recognizes the colossal difficulties Russia faced during your lifetime.

R.A.Clio *adds some light marbles for that. The scale is balancing about evenly.*

Justice: It is the decision of this Court that you are not ready for either Heaven or Hell. You will therefore spend time in Purgatory Rehab. Normally that would include doing Penance, but your life in Russia was enough of that. However, you will do Community Service as an advisor to the present Russian government. See if you can help them rein in the new plutocrats – and deal wisely with Ukraine. You can bring along your Memoirs.

<u>R.A.Clio</u> *presents Khrushchev with the 3 thick volumes. He is delighted to finally see the published product.*

<u>Justice</u>: You will also take Anger Management classes – along with some of your peers here. And you will spend as much time in meditation as it takes for you to realize that God is not a Communist.

*Brief Recess*

<u>Justice</u>: The Court calls Lyndon Johnson.

<u>LBJ</u> *stands before* <u>Justice</u> *and* <u>Clio's</u> *scales.*

<u>R.A.Clio</u>: Throughout all your years as a public servant, you worked harder than anyone to 'make things better for folks.'

*She puts a handful of light marbles in the Right Pan.*

The amount of legislation passed for your Great Society and War on Poverty programs was unprecedented.

*She puts a light marble in the Right Pan for each of these laws. It takes a <u>long</u> time. When finished, the Right Pan is full and resting on the floor.*

Throughout your career, you were known as a wheeler-dealer, who did not hesitate to cross the line.

*Several dark marbles. Right Pan lifts slightly.*

But more often than not, this was done to achieve necessary consensus among people with divergent views.

*Light marbles. Right Pan is back on floor.*

Your greatest achievement was passing Civil Rights legislation that outlawed discrimination and segregation. To do this, you had to rise above the racism of your native Texas. Though many of your southern colleagues never forgave you, de-segregation eventually enabled the South to rejoin the Union economically. Your wisdom and courage are duly noted.

*Empties the bowl of light marbles, some of which spill out of the Right Pan.*

Unfortunately, your narrow view of the world caused the escalation of the Vietnam War into one of the greatest tragedies in U.S. History. It almost destroyed Vietnam, tore apart the USA, and ended your political career.

*Several handfuls of dark marbles in Wrong Pan. The Right Pan rises.*

You fell into this trap because you were unable to see beyond the prevailing American view of the Cold War.

*Empties bowl of dark marbles into Wrong Pan. Some spill out. The scales are equally balanced.*

Justice: Mr. President, your deeds of commission are many, with the good and evil equally balanced. You, too, are not ready for Heaven – or Hell. So you will also spend time in Purgatory Rehab. But because you had a comfortable life in a country with no serious obstacles, you must also do penance. You will spend much of your time in solitary confinement. Your only company will be your neighbors, with whom you will share meals. Bobby Kennedy will be next door...

LBJ *groans.*

<u>Justice</u>:...and Khrushchev will be down the hall. It is hoped that your interactions – especially with Comrade Khrushchev – will widen your view of the world. Reading Nehru's books and De Gaulle's Memoirs will also help.

<u>Churchill</u>: What about <u>my</u> books?

<u>Justice</u>: Only after you've revised them.

*She hands the books by Nehru and De Gaulle to <u>LBJ</u>.*

You will also do Community Service. Your skill at achieving consensus is much needed by the present U.S. Congress. So you will have carte blanche to do whatever it takes to get them to stop bickering and do their job.

<u>LBJ</u>: (*grinning hugely*) And you say I can do <u>anything</u>?!

<u>Justice</u>: Yep. The problem is such that we will look the other way.

<u>LBJ</u>: (*obviously delighted*) When do I start?

<u>Justice</u>: As soon as you finish the Anger Management classes you and Comrade Khrushchev will be in.

<u>LBJ</u> *and* <u>Khrushchev</u> *look at each other warily – but with curiosity rather than hostility.*

<u>Justice</u>: And while in Solitary, you will hopefully realize that God is neither a Capitalist nor a Texan.

*Brief Recess*

<u>Justice</u>: The Court finally calls Sir Winston Churchill, Prime Minister of England.

Churchill *faces The Scale and corrects* Justice.
That should be Prime Minister of Great Britain.

Justice *shrugs.* Prime Minister of Britain.

Churchill *growls.*

R.A.Clio: As everyone knows, you rallied the English People to heroically resist Hitler, and led them in their finest hour.

*Light marbles.*

You helped General De Gaulle save France.

*Light marbles.*

You forged alliances with America and Russia. Together you defeated the Nazis.

*Light marbles.*

You wrote books about all this, which won you the Nobel Prize in Literature. Richly deserved for rescuing the English language from Shakespeare's ranting.

*Light marbles.*

Although your books are a great read, they are unfortunately biased toward the view that you won the war single-handedly.

*Dark marbles.*

You participated as an equal in determining the postwar settlement, thus maintaining Britain's status as a world power.

*Light marbles.*

And then you played the traditional British game of divide-and-balance, sowing the seeds of dissension between America and Russia, and fanning the flames of the Cold War.

*Dark marbles.*

Your prestige and British aura made your 'Iron Curtain' speech sound like the 11th Commandment. Much of President Johnson's view of Russia stems from this.

*Dark marbles.*

Meanwhile, you clung to the Empire and retarded Indian Independence. You allowed millions to die in the Bengal Famine. You imprisoned Nehru and his colleagues and encouraged Jinnah and the Muslim League, thus contributing to the Partition and establishment of Pakistan.

*Many dark marbles*

All your life you had the comforts and privileges of being an English aristocrat. You used your advantages to make the Empire a vast playground for your own aggrandizement.

*Many, many dark marbles*

And then, when you finally turned over the Empire to the Americans, you saddled them with the worst attitudes of imperialism.

*Reaches for more dark marbles – but the bowl is already empty.*

Justice: The Court finds itself in a dilemma. The avalanche of Dark has almost buried the Light. But all that you did was in order to save the Empire. Since you, in fact, personify that Empire, what is on trial here is the British Empire itself.

That is way above our pay-grade! So we called in our Bosses.

Churchill: Of course! God and I will work it out.

Justice: Nope. God doesn't want you. S/He is not an Englishman.

Churchill *harrumphs angrily.*

Justice: The Devil, however, looks forward to your presence in Hell. S/He has often inspired the British Empire, and looks forward to discussing your mutual creation.

Churchill: *(indignantly)* The Devil is NOT an Englishman!

Justice: During your life, you experienced all the positive attributes of the British Empire. And yes – there were many. But now it is time for you to experience the dark side. The Devil's Advocate informs me that her boss has arranged a prolonged visit to India under the Raj. But you will be Indian – not British.

Churchill *is speechless.*

Justice: But the Devil has entrance requirements. First, you must take the Anger Management class with Khrushchev and LBJ. Mr. Nehru has generously agreed to be the teacher.

Nehru, *with a gleam of satisfaction, does a gracious 'namaste' at* Churchill, *whose indignation knows no bounds.*

R.A.Clio: And you must also revise your books about World War II. Your wonderful writing has convinced the world that you won the War all by yourself.

General De Gaulle has volunteered to be your editor. He has asked Mr. Nehru to assist.

Churchill *swallows his cigar.*

Justice *pounds her gavel.* Cosmic Justice has been served. The Court of Purgatory is hereby adjourned!

*Minions from Heaven and Hell lead the subdued statesmen off to their respective fates.*

Justice *takes off her diadem and rubs her head.* Whew! All that Enlightenment gets heavy after awhile.

Clio *also removes her mortarboard.* Indeed! And constantly correcting erroneous World History gets old after awhile. *She smiles dryly.* Pardon the pun.

Devil's Advocate and Guardian Angel *remove horns and halo, respectively.*

G.A.: These things do tend to stereotype us.

D.A.: Maybe next time we should switch?

G.A.: Hmm. That might be interesting.

Clio: Better check with the Boss first.

All *walk over to vacated jury box, sit down wearily, lean back and relax.*

<u>Devil's Advocate</u> *kicks off her shoes, conjures up a bottle of vintage champagne, and fills the crystal flutes which appear in each of their hands.*

<u>Justice</u> *raises her glass.* To Truth: Past, Present, Future.

<u>All:</u> To Truth!

*They drain their champagne glasses, then throw them into the fireplace which has suddenly appeared at the other end of the room.*

*Fade Out*

# EPILOGUE

*The final Chorus of the Bach B minor Mass begins very softly.*
 *Dona nobis Pacem*
 *Grant us Peace*
 *Dona nobis Pacem*

*Fade In.*

*The Courtroom is gone.*

*A single spotlight illuminates* <u>Justice</u>, *standing mid-stage, her scale in one hand, her sword in the other.*
 *Dona nobis Pacem*
 *Grant us Peace*
 *Dona nobis Pacem*

*More voices, high and low, join in.*

<u>Justice:</u> Yes, grant us Peace.

But is Peace possible without Justice?

And when so few have so much, and so many have not enough, can there be Justice?
 *Dona nobis Pacem*

*The counterpoint becomes complex.*

The men who were on trial here in Purgatory had much Power. Did they use it to pursue justice? Or did they abuse their power?
    *Dona nobis Pacem*

*The music gradually crescendos.*

Ultimately, did they get what they deserved?

And – when it's your turn – will you?

*A high, true note from a trumpet echoes the question.*
    *Dona nobis Pacem*
    *Grant us Peace*
    *Dona nobis pacem*

*The light on* Justice *slowly dims.*

*The B minor Mass finally resolves into a hopeful B major Amen.*

# ACKNOWLEDGEMENTS

My understanding of the people in this book was greatly enhanced by the fact that all of them wrote books about their careers. Reading them provided many interesting 'conversations'.

Winston Churchill
*The Second World War* (6 volumes)
*The History of the English-Speaking Peoples* (4 volumes)

Charles De Gaulle
*The Complete War Memoirs*
*Memoirs of Hope: Renewal and Endeavor*

Lyndon Johnson
*The Vantage Point: Perspectives of the Presidency 1963 – 1969*

Nikita Khrushchev
*Memoirs of Khrushchev* (3 huge volumes)

Jawaharlal Nehru
*Autobiography*
*The Discovery of India*
*Glimpses of World History*
*Selected Works of Jawaharlal Nehru* (Many, many volumes)

# AFTERWORD

Dr. Kirsten E.A. Borg grew up in the menacing and perplexing shadow of the Cold War. She witnessed its demise with relief, but views with dismay all the rubble it left behind. She has often wondered if the Cold War was inevitable, and whether it might have ended sooner – and with less devastation. As always, she has searched diligently for answers, has sometimes been surprised by what she discovered, and occasionally had to change her mind about its major players.

Dr. Borg lives with her husband and daughter in Kansas City and Door County, Wisconsin. She is a 'retired' teacher who has taught many subjects to many kinds of students in many ways and places (including Academia, Russia, and the Public Schools). She is an engaging speaker, and is available to meet with bookclubs and various community groups.

For more information about Dr. Borg and her books, see her website at www.booksbykeab.com